Trying Out

To some people, the Great Wave may be just "some crummy cafe," but I certainly don't feel that way. "Jessica this is — uh — Alicia Marin," Steve says, glancing down at the sheet before he tells her my name. That's how hard he's trying to pretend we hardly know each other.

"Hello, Alicia," Jessica says warmly. She has a very soothing voice. "What are you going to sing for us today?" she asks. She has a very calming effect on me, and I realize that even if I'm lousy, she's too nice to say anything cruel.

"It's called *My City Song*."

"Well, anytime you're ready." I'm as ready as I'll ever be, so I plunge right in.

"The boys on the corner, talkin'
They whistle as I pass through,
But I don't look, I keep on walkin'
On my block, that's what nice girls do. . . ."

Surprisingly enough, my voice doesn't sound shaky. In fact, it fills the room. A look of relief crosses Steve's face and Jessica Flynn leans forward.

Best of all, I discover I am actually enjoying myself.

Other Apple paperbacks
you will enjoy:

Adorable Sunday
by Marlene Fanta Shyer

The Trouble with Soap
by Margery Cuyler

A Season of Secrets
by Alison Cragin Herzig &
Jane Lawrence Mali

Friends Are Like That
by Patricia Hermes

Starstruck

Marisa Gioffre

AN
APPLE®
PAPERBACK

SCHOLASTIC INC.
New York Toronto London Auckland Sydney

I wish to thank Lynn Ahrens for generously permitting me to include lyrics from the songs she composed for the ABC AfterSchool Special Series production of *Starstruck*: *"My City Song," "The Great American Hit,"* and *"Gonna' Make My Dreams Come True,"* music and lyrics by Lynn Ahrens, copyright 1981, Hillsdale Music, Inc.

Also thanks to Ann Martin and Brenda Bowen for their patience and encouragement and to Ann Tobias for her extra efforts.

Library of Congress Cataloging in Publication Data
Gioffre, Marisa.
    Starstruck.
    Summary: Alicia's dream of becoming a professional singer clashes with her mother's plans to get her a bookkeeping job at the factory where she works.
    1. Children's stories, American. [1. Singers — Fiction. 2. Occupations — Fiction. 3. Mothers and daughters — Fiction] I. Title.
PZ7.G4392St 1985   [Fic]   85-2153
ISBN 0-590-33797-1

ISBN 0-590-33797-1

12 11 10 9 8 7 6 5 4 3 2 1   8   5 6 7 8 9/8 0/9
                Printed in the U.S.A.   06

for Giovanna
   and for
      Jomana Bikaii, Sabra Camp, Beirut

Chapter 1

How pathetic can you get? My first big break and I can't even tune my guitar, that's how badly my hands are shaking. If I'm this nervous while I'm alone in my room, how crazed will I be when I get to my audition at the Great Wave? I'm afraid I already know the answer. At best, I'll be a borderline basket case. At worst, they'll have to cart me off the stage in a straitjacket.

I wonder if Linda Ronstadt was a wreck before *her* first professional audition. I'll have to remember to ask her after we become chummy. Even if Linda and I never become fast friends, there'll be plenty of opportunities to compare notes on the subject; for instance, at the party following the Grammy Awards or backstage at Madison Square Garden on a night we're both appearing at a benefit concert. By then, I probably won't even remember what it feels like to have stage fright. Who knows? I might even laugh when I look back on today.

When Papa was alive, we would take walks through Central Park on days he wasn't working. I'd tell him how I planned to become a famous singer-songwriter when I grew up. He never made me feel like it was a crazy dream. With Mama, it's another story. One night I confided my plans in her as we were clearing away the dinner dishes. "If things go according to schedule, I should have a gold record by the time I'm twenty-one," I said. She raised her eyebrows. That should have been sufficient warning. But like a fool, I continued. "Maybe I'll have even won a Grammy by then."

"Why not, Alicia? And maybe tonight when we turn on the news, we'll find out the mayor has sold Manhattan back to the Indians," she answered.

Ordinarily Mama doesn't have much sense of humor. That's because she worries so much, especially since Papa died four years ago. The truck my father was driving crashed on a New Jersey highway one night. It's still hard for me to talk about it.

Anyway, Mama may never have joked all the time like her sister Yolanda, but some of her put-downs can be pretty funny. I'm the first to admit it, even though being on the receiving end of them can hurt like crazy. I've finally learned to never let on that her wisecracks get to me. If I sulk she immediately becomes exasperated. "Alicia, don't be so sensitive," she'll lecture me. Then she'll quote my Grandmother Esperanza: "Only the rich can afford to be thin-skinned."

Grandmother Esperanza has dozens of sayings like these, which she constantly rattles off. To hear Mama tell it, Grandma's pearls of wisdom have made her a minor celebrity in the *barrio* in old San Juan where she lives and where Mama grew up. Since most of her mottoes lose a lot in translation, it's hard to know how seriously to take Mama's claim. One thing is certain however; Esperanza Santiago's words made a lasting impression on her daughter Inez. Even though Mama moved to New York City eighteen years ago, hardly a week goes by when she doesn't spring one of Grandmother Esperanza's quotes on me.

The little clock on my bureau says ten to four. It's almost time to leave for the audition. Steve will murder me if I'm late. He's the reason I'm in this mess in the first place. He works at the Great Wave coffee house and he arranged the tryout for me.

Steve's my pal at John Adams High School. Back in junior high school, my homeroom teacher had me take the entrance exam to John Adams and I passed it without any trouble. John Adams is one of those special high schools where the students come from all over the city. The classes are harder there than in most public schools, and I was afraid it would be real stuck-up, but it isn't like that at all. Some of the kids, Steve for instance, have parents who could easily afford to send them to private schools. Only their families wanted them to go to a school where they could receive a decent education and also get a broader view of life. That was true in the case of Steve's parents, anyhow.

Steve and I have been buddies since our freshman year when we were in *Guys and Dolls* together. Come to think of it, Steve's my *best* buddy, although it's strictly platonic between us. Platonic, not to be confused wtih harmonious. The general consensus among our friends is that it's a rare day when Stephen Adlai Lewis and Alicia Consuelo Marin don't disagree about something.

After our last class today, Steve must have known I was having second thoughts about the audition because he said to me, "Just remember Marshall Brickman's famous line."

I was confused. "That nerdy guy who sits behind me in trigonometry?" I asked. I couldn't remember Marshall ever opening his mouth, much less saying anything famous.

Steve looked appalled. It's the expression he gets when he has a hard time believing I am actually as ignorant as I appear to be. "Not Marshall *Bromberg*, nitwit. Marshall *Brickman*. Woody Allen's lifelong collaborator. The genius who wrote all his best films with him before branching out on his own."

Besides being an expert on every Broadway musical ever produced, Steve can tell you who wrote and directed every film that's been released in the past ten years. That's because he reads *Variety* from cover to cover each week. *Variety* is the show business trade paper. It doesn't tell you anything juicy like which stars are going around together. *Variety* mostly prints boring stuff like how much a film grossed in Toledo, Ohio last month. Except Steve doesn't think that's boring. He finds it fascinating. He has so much information like this at his finger tips I'm sure he started reading *Variety* when he was a baby. It must be one of the reasons he was able to talk himself into his emcee job at the Great Wave.

"Okay, so what did this Marshall Brickman say?" I was eager to get home and change. If I couldn't bowl over the Great Wave's owner with my talent, I figured I could at least look presentable.

"He said that eighty percent of life is showing up." Steve's voice had the tone our English teacher uses when he's quoting Shakespeare.

"That's it?"

"Yes. Isn't it an absolutely brilliant insight?"

"I don't get it," I answered truthfully.

"He's saying you have to be willing to put yourself on the line . . . that you can't hit a home run, unless you get up to bat."

"Last time I got up to bat, I nearly got beaned by the pitcher's spit ball," I reminded him. Baseball is definitely not my thing.

Steve sighed and his blue-gray eyes looked melancholy.

I hate it when he acts hurt because we're not on the same wavelength, as if I'm misunderstanding him on purpose.

"Why don't we just drop it, Marin?" he retorted. Steve always calls me by my last name. He claims it's a nonsexist thing to do. I think he just prefers the way Marin sounds. Alicia is old-fashioned but Marin is breezier, more contemporary.

With departure time approaching, I can see Brickman's point of view a lot more clearly. For starters, showing up takes courage. Particularly when your guitar has a flat C sharp and a hopeless G. Linda Ronstadt might have had knots in her stomach the first time she sang for strangers, but I'll bet anything her guitar was in tune. Get a grip on yourself, Marin, I tell myself. Keep this up and you'll never make it out the door. It's now or never, I realize. I zip my guitar case in one quick motion, no small accomplishment when you consider my hand tremor. Then I look in the mirror one last time. To be honest, I look flushed. I feel my forehead. It's warm. Maybe I'm developing a fever.

It's too late to cancel out, so just make the best of it, I tell myself. I remember what

Papa used to tell me: "You'll never know if you can do something, Alicia *mi amor*, unless you try." He always gave me pep talks when I was afraid. I hurry through the apartment, double lock the door, and rush down the stairs.

The weather happens to be great, something I'd failed to notice earlier. Very sunny, but with a breeze, and hardly any humidity in the air. As usual, Mrs. Reuben is at her post. She's this really nice Jewish lady who lives in the ground floor apartment of the building next to mine. She must be about seventy by now. Ever since she retired a few years ago, she spends most of her waking hours checking out the block from the window of her apartment. If you want a rundown on what is happening in our neighborhood, she's definitely the person to talk to.

"You look very original today, Alicia," she comments as I reach the stoop. "Where are you going?"

"Uptown," I answer vaguely. It's funny — if most adults say you look original, what they really mean is you look weird. But I know Mrs. Reuben is paying me a compliment. Ordinarily, I would stop and talk with her, but as I look up the street, I notice the First Avenue bus approaching. I decide to make a dash for it.

The doors have already closed by the time I reach the bus. I pound on them. "Have a heart, mister," I plead to the driver, hoping he can hear through the glass. I'm usually not that aggressive. After mulling over my request for what seems an eternity, he decides to let me in.

I take it as a good omen. By the time I thank him, fumble for the correct change, and find a seat, we've already passed Silvieri's fish store. According to the outdoor clock that hangs over the store, it's only thirteen minutes after four. If traffic isn't too heavy, there's an outside chance I won't be late. But I'm not holding my breath.

Marshall Brickman may be very perceptive and all, but I have a hunch he never had to depend on New York City public transportation to get around. Because if that were the case, his famous line would have been, "eighty percent of life is showing up — on time."

Chapter 2

Sure enough, traffic along First Avenue is hopelessly snarled. It's twenty minutes later and we're only on 23rd Street. The Great Wave is a full forty blocks away. Too bad I don't have enough stamina to walk. I'd get there twice as fast. The worst thing about crawling along like this is that it gives me time to brood about all the things that can go wrong this afternoon. Just last week, our guidance teacher, Mr. Aarons, told the class that all adolescents suffer from sharp mood swings and feelings of severe self-doubt. "When you're sixteen, periods of deep depression are par for the course," he assured us.

I don't deny I've become even moodier lately, but I've always been what Steve terms "mercurial." Papa was the same way, although even he wasn't in my league.

Steve summed it up once: some are born to party and some are born to brood. He once told me I raised brooding to an art form. Of course he was wisecracking, but to tell you the truth I didn't mind. I think he meant I have an imagination that won't quit. Imagination is considered a positive trait, at least in theory. In reality, once you're over ten, having an imagination makes you suspect, even among your close friends. Take Robin Fox, for instance. For the most part, Robin's okay. We started hanging out together last year when we were in the same homeroom. She's got this straight, naturally shiny chestnut hair. Her posture's so good she can balance her school books on her head. I like her because she's always game. By that I mean she likes to do things instead of just moping around.

But every now and then, Robin will zap you with one of her famous left-handed compliments. Yesterday at lunch, she said, "Alicia, you have such a vivid imagination. You'll never have to worry about being lonely." It wasn't so much her words; it was the sticky way she lingered over every syllable in "Imagination." Having an active imagination doesn't necessarily mean you're a flake. I know Papa didn't make me feel that way. But try convincing practical souls like Robin of that. It's an uphill battle.

Compared with my mother's views on the subject though, Robin's swipes are nothing. My mother doesn't just observe that someone has an imagination. She accuses them of it. Once I heard her say that Aunt Yolanda "suffered" from a big imagination. If you didn't know what the word meant, you'd swear she was discussing some horrible disease.

Right now, as the bus crawls along, I'm trying to decide what would be worse: If I botch up my song during the audition this afternoon, or if I open my mouth to sing and absolutely no sound comes out. It *could* happen. Mr. Aarons says that extreme stress can trigger a hysterical paralysis. To tell the truth, I think developing a hysterical paralysis wouldn't be so bad. For one thing, everybody would feel sorry for me. And Jessica Flynn, who owns the Great Wave, might even let me audition again someday when I've got it more together.

The Great Wave is sort of funky and real classy at the same time, if that makes any sense. To hear Steve tell it, it's one of the best showcases in town for young performers. The pay isn't great and you have to wait on tables between sets. But Steve swears record producers and talent agents cover the shows all the time. When I pinned him down, he admitted they showed up only occasionally. "But it still beats singing on your stoop, Marin," Steve pointed out. No argument there.

On the night I checked out the Great Wave, Jessica seemed pretty nice. She's this real attractive black woman. Steve told me she'd been raised in Louisiana. When she was about twenty, she took off for Paris where she became a cabaret singer. Since she returned to the States and bought the coffee house, Jessica's main interest has been in promoting young talent. You can count on getting a fair shake from her. But she is no pushover, that much is clear.

If I bomb out today, I'm praying Jessica will just let me slink away quietly. I'd die if she made a cutting remark in front of everybody. Something like, "Young lady, if I were you, I'd be grateful the composer isn't around to hear how you mangled that song." If she said that, I'd never have the guts to tell her the truth. Namely, that the song I'd mangled was one of my own. Anyway, she'd find out soon enough. I'm sure the newspapers would mention it in my obituary once my body had been fished out of the East River.

Aren't you letting things get a little out of hand, I ask myself, imagining what your obituary will say? I mean if I'm going to daydream, why not fantasize about something pleasant — like a standing ovation.

Suddenly, I notice the street sign. I'm practically there, and I scramble to get off the bus. Manhattan is a funny place. It's like eleven different towns laid out side by side. That's how much neighborhoods can differ. My neighborhood, the East Village, is pretty poor compared to some sections, but in my opinion it's still got a lot going for it. I like it because people of all different nationalities live there. In my building alone, we have Puerto Ricans, Dominicans, Ukranians, Russians, blacks, and a modern dance student at New York University who grew up in South Dakota.

The neighborhood I'm in now, however, the Upper East Side, is a little too slick for my taste. On the corner is a unisex clothing boutique. Everything in it costs a fortune. Next is one of those gourmet take-out joints that sells twenty different kinds of quiche. And right next to that is the place where my fate will be decided.

I'm late. Steve told me auditions seldom run on schedule. I'm hoping this one is no different. Now that the zero hour is here, I remember Steve's final advice: "The main thing, Marin, is to *act* confident — even if inside, you're a mass of quivering jelly." Steve's right. So what if I feel like pure jelly? There's no reason to let Jessica Flynn in on that fact. I toss my head back defiantly, the way movie stars do when the chips are down. Then I march toward the Great Wave and swing open the door.

Chapter 3

Me and my big ideas. I didn't have to wait to get on stage to make a fool of myself. I managed to do it the minute I walked in the door. I'd pushed it open so hard it banged back with a thud — smack in the middle of someone else's audition.

Steve, who is sitting beside Jessica, glares at me. My heart drops when I notice Jessica frowning as she sizes me up. Some great first impression. I mouth the words, "I'm sorry." To my relief, she smiles, as if to say it's no big deal. Steve, however, still looks disapproving. So much for counting on him. He's assisting Jessica with the auditions. Now he gets up and walks around, looking very official, a clipboard in his hand, a pencil behind his ear. Sometimes he can be a real pain.

Meanwhile, the guy whose audition I

disrupted is still pouring his heart out. He's tall and wiry and very intense. The ballad he's singing sounds pretty flowery and a piano player is backing him up with some very fancy chords.

> "Love can be conversation,
> Bringing us close together,
> Helping us find each other."

Truthfully, I'm not impressed. But then he'd probably think my stuff is weird — too ethnic or something.

Steve ambles over to me in this very casual manner. He decided beforehand it would be a good idea if we pretended to be just acquaintances rather than fast friends. That way Jessica would consider his endorsement of me an objective opinion. I don't know why he assumed she'd depend on his judgment because she hardly seems the type of person who needs help making up her mind.

"Great entrance," Steve mutters to me under his breath as he checks my name off his list. I knew he wouldn't be able to resist rubbing it in.

"You told me to walk in like I own the place," I say in defense.

"Like you own it, not like you're out to demolish it."

"Am I late?" I ask. Anything to change the subject.

"You just made it. Calm down."

That's easy enough for him to say. Suddenly it's hit me hard. Eighty percent of life may be showing up, but it's the other twenty percent that really matters — what you do once you get there.

Steve realizes I'm a wreck and takes pity on me. "Just sing like you do when you're at home, Marin, and you can't miss." Not only does he say this with conviction, but he smiles at me. Steve is no Robert Redford, but he does have an excellent smile. Even Robin agrees. To be fair about it, Steve has other nice qualities. Like he never snickers when I carry on about becoming a famous singer-songwriter. He's one of the few people who takes my ambition seriously. To be perfectly blunt, he's the *only* person who takes it seriously. I certainly hope today doesn't change his mind.

The guy who was singing a moment ago is already on his way out. "She'll let me know — I like that," I overhear him griping to his accompanist. From the sound of it, J.F. has given him the brush-off.

"Don't sweat it," his accompanist replies. "It's just some crummy cafe, not a big Broadway musical." Before I can mull that one over, Jessica calls me forward. I take it one step at a time and manage to reach the stage without knocking anything over.

To some people, the Great Wave may be just "some crummy cafe," but I certainly don't feel that way. "Jessica, this is — uh — Alicia Marin," Steve says, glancing down at the sheet before he tells her my name. That's how hard he's trying to pretend we hardly know each other. What a character. If he keeps up this routine, I swear I'll crack up.

"Hello, Alicia," Jessica says warmly. She has a very soothing voice. "What are you going to sing for us today?" she asks. She has a very calming effect on me, and I realize that even if I'm lousy, she's too nice to say anything cruel.

"It's called *My City Song*."

"Well, anytime you're ready." I'm as ready as I'll ever be, so I plunge right in.

"The boys on the corner, talkin'
They whistle as I pass through,
But I don't look, I keep on walkin'
On my block, that's what nice girls do...."

Surprisingly enough, my voice doesn't sound shaky. In fact, it fills the room. A look of relief crosses Steve's face and Jessica Flynn leans forward. Not a lot, but enough to convey the impression I'm not boring her to death. I unwind a little.

"But in my heart, I know they're shy,
That's why they come on so strong,
And I sing
La la la le lo.
My city song."

Believe it or not, Jessica seems even more attentive. Steve is starting to look very pleased with himself. Best of all, I discover I am actually enjoying myself.

"Rumble of the subway, passin' by
Green banana man, you hear his cry,
Pigeons on the roof, too fat to fly
I can hear the music,
City, let me use it. . . ."

By the time I finish, I'm really cooking and I've stopped checking on their reactions. But after singing my last, "la la la le lo, my city song," I look up and see that Steve is grinning. Jessica's reaction is more reserved, but when she says, "Good song, Alicia," it's with real enthusiasm.

"Where did you find it?" she asks.

"I wrote it," I answer.

"Have you written many songs?"

"A few here and there," I mumble idiotically. Suddenly I feel excruciatingly shy.

It's funny how much more comfortable I felt when I was singing, than I do now answering questions. Fortunately, Steve comes to my rescue. "She's written dozens of them. Ballads, up-tempo stuff, and all of it's unique." I stand there staring at my feet. Compliments always make me squirm.

"You'll have a chance to try your songs out here," Jessica says.

Is this really happening to me?

"I have an opening for five nights a week," she continues matter-of-factly. "That sound good to you?"

"Sounds great." *Why can't I be more eloquent?*

"Remember you'll be singing only about one-tenth of the time. The rest you'll be waiting on tables. Have you ever waitressed before?"

I'd forgotten about that part of the deal. "No," I admit.

Jessica is silent. She must be having second thoughts about hiring me. I knew it was too good to be true.

To my relief, she says, "You'll learn."

I wish I could share her confidence. Obviously my noisy entrance has failed to alert her to the fact that I'm terminally clumsy.

"Talk to Larry Egans, our Assistant Manager. He'll set up a time to brief you."

"Uh-huh," I reply brilliantly. I continue to stand there like a dummy until I notice Steve gesturing to me to get off the stage. Apparently, Jessica's last sentence had been my exit cue. But in my shock at being hired I didn't pick up on it. I clear the stage with all the grace of a robot as Steve calls for the next auditionee.

When he meets me outside a few minutes later I finally emerge from my daze. "Someone is actually going to pay me to sing my songs!"

"I knew Jessica would like you," Steve answers. His tone implies his confidence in me had never failed. He could have fooled me, but I decide to let it pass.

"You're on your way, Marin," he adds. "Today the Great Wave, tomorrow Madison Square Garden." Steve is as excited as I am. This makes me feel I've been a little hard on him. What's fair is fair. Not only did he set up the audition, he shamed me into not copping out.

"Play your cards right and I'll dedicate

my first album to you." That's as close as I can come to saying thank you.

"I'm really touched, Marin." I guess that's as close as he can come to saying you're welcome. "Wait till the kids at school hear. Especially Robin." I stop short.

"What's the matter?" Steve asks. Steve usually takes my abrupt mood changes in stride, but this time, he looks genuinely concerned.

"Wait till my mother hears," I blurt out.

Chapter 4

I remain immobilized by the prospect of confronting my mother. "I thought she wanted you to get a summer job," Steve says.

"She does, but not necessarily this kind of job," I explain. "Besides, she hates it when I do things behind her back."

"You never told her about the audition?"

I shake my head. Given the odds against my being hired, I didn't see the point in thrashing it out with her beforehand.

"Even if she is annoyed, Marin, I'm sure she won't stand in your way. Not once she realizes how much it means to you."

I have to laugh. My mother is not a staunch supporter of my show biz aspirations. But no matter how often I explain this to Steve, he has great difficulty grasping the fact.

It's because his own parents are so different. Mr. Aarons would definitely label them "permissive," while he'd categorize my mother as an "authoritarian" type. Steve's mother and father read all the Dr. Spock books before their kids were even born. That should give you some idea of the kind of parents they are. Mr. Lewis is a labor lawyer. Steve claims his dad is heartbroken that Steve has shown no interest in becoming a union organizer or something equally noble. But at least Mr. Lewis keeps his opinions to himself. If Steve broke the news to them tomorrow that he wanted to become a camel herder, his parents might not be wild about the idea but their only comment would be, "That's nice, dear." No wonder Steve can't understand my dilemma. He has no idea what it's like to live with an absolute dictator. Somehow or other, I'll have to make my mother see the light. I pull myself together, and we continue towards Second Avenue and the downtown bus stop.

It's nearly six and the streets are crowded with people hurrying home from their jobs. Unless my mother has had to work overtime at the factory, she'll already be home by now. It won't help my case any that I'm still out. Mama is strict about things like that, although my Aunt Yolanda keeps reminding her that she's not in San Juan any longer, and that girls are raised differently here.

I hope Aunt Yolanda is with Mama right now. Since Yo lives just down the block from us, she hangs out in our apartment a lot. Although they bicker all the time, Aunt Yo is one of the few people who can make my mother laugh. I love having her around. Mostly because she's fun and very understanding. But also because she keeps Mama on her toes and that takes some of the pressure off me.

We've reached the bus stop. Suddenly, my guitar seems heavy. It's so old it's practically an antique. The strings need replacing, but the body is so beautifully crafted, I'll never want another. It's made from fine-grained wood, the kind you hardly ever see anymore. But even if the guitar weren't so beautiful, I'd keep it forever. It used to belong to Papa, and one of my earliest memories is of him singing Puerto Rican folk songs to me, while he strummed.

Fortunately, the problem strings didn't sound too awful to me this afternoon. To make sure I'm not kidding myself, I ask Steve for his opinion. "The sound was passable," he says. "But you really should buy new strings for it," he adds once we're on the bus and settled in our seats. I frown. It's not the first time he's made that suggestion.

"That costs money," I point out.

"Think of it as a career investment. Sometimes you have to spend money in order to make money."

"In order to spend money, first you have to have some," I snap.

"Okay, let's drop it."

I didn't mean to jump down his throat, but Steve can be so dense sometimes. I hate it when I have to remind him that, unlike his family, my mother and I have very little money to spend. Steve's father rakes it in as a lawyer, and his mother also makes a good salary as a textbook editor. I don't know how much they earn a year, but I'd probably consider it a small fortune. Once I heard Steve's father comment that unlike a lot of his old law school buddies, he still votes Democrat, even though his tax bracket was now solidly Republican.

I don't know what Mama thinks about politics, but her tax bracket is anything but Republican. She works as an operator in a clothing factory, same as Aunt Yo. She ranks with the best of them when it comes to stretching her paycheck. But there are limits to how far her salary can go. I consider myself lucky when I can afford a pair of crazy patterned leg warmers. Last year, when Steve got great grades at the end of sophomore year, his parents gave him a new speaker system. That should give a rough idea of the difference in our economic status.

Traffic moving downtown isn't as slow as it had been the other way. When I get off the bus, it's only a short walk from the stop to the railroad flat where my mom and I live. Our block is one of the nicest in the neighborhood. A lot of the buildings are freshly painted, a few in pastel colors, dusty rose and pale turquoise. They remind me of the area in old San Juan where Grandmother Esperanza lives. We even have a couple of full-grown trees and a wall-sized mural that was painted a few years ago.

Our apartment is small, but I like it because it is very sunny. The best part is that I have my own room. A few of my cousins have to sleep three in a bed, so they consider me lucky. I remind them that I'm an only child. That isn't so lucky. Not in my book, anyhow. Sometimes I wonder why Mama and Papa didn't have other children.

Maybe they decided that there was too little money to go around, and they wanted to be sure that I'd have enough to eat and decent clothes to wear.

If some of my cousins envy me, I wonder what they'd think if they ever saw Steve's house. They'd probably think it was a mansion. Mr. and Mrs. Lewis own this huge brownstone off lower Fifth Avenue. That's one of the richest sections of Greenwich Village. Although it's only a ten-minute walk from my place, going there is like stepping into a different world. Not that it's fixed up fancy or anything. His parents have very simple tastes. Which is nice because with its huge windows, high ceilings, and fantastic woodwork, the house is too beautiful to clutter up with a lot of junk.

It kills me the way Steve takes his house for granted. Maybe it's understandable since he's lived there his whole life. As soon as I make it big, I plan to buy one just like it. And believe me, I will *never* take it for granted. When I'm on an exhausting road tour, knowing I have a beautiful home to return to will mean a lot to me.

The only thing spoiling it is that my father won't be there to appreciate it with me. It's hard to believe four years have already passed since he died. For a long time I blocked him out of my mind because thinking about him hurt too much. It still makes me sad, of course, but now I like remembering him and recalling his face, especially his smile. It was even more terrific than Steve's. It would crinkle at the edges of his mouth like he was sharing this special secret with just you alone. Then it would broaden into a wide grin. Once I showed Robin this picture of him that I always carry around in my wallet and she said he was "dazzling." And as I pointed out earlier, she's the last person in the world to gush.

Papa's family moved to New York City from Puerto Rico when he was eight. He told me once how he and Mom got together. Back when he was eighteen, the night flight to San Juan cost only forty-five dollars. His parents scraped up the air fare for him as a graduation present, so he could visit his aunt and uncle. One day he was walking in the *piazza* with his uncle when he saw this beautiful young girl come out of church. "Forget about it," his uncle warned him. "That's Esperanza Santiago's daughter." It seems that very few prospective boyfriends had passed Grandma Esperanza's inspection. But that didn't scare Papa. He had originally planned to stay in San Juan only a few weeks. Instead he didn't return to Manhattan until Labor Day.

The next summer he earned his own air fare to San Juan. And this time when he came back to New York, he brought Mama with him. That past winter, he had been playing with a little band on weekends. I guess Papa must have painted a pretty rosy picture of what their life would be like in the States. Mama never said anything outright, but I've always had the impression that reality turned out to be a big letdown.

After I was born, the band broke up and Papa started his own group. They'd get a few gigs here and there, but they weren't exactly swamped with bookings. In order to earn a living, he did everything from wait on tables to drive a truck. For a while he even operated an elevator in a fancy Park Avenue apartment building. I remember his coming home one night and announcing that money definitely did not make people happy. He said he had never seen such a sour bunch of faces as those of the Park Avenue tenants who rode up and down in that marble elevator.

I realize now how much he must have hated all those dumb jobs. But he never complained. Instead he tried to make a game out of them. He was always telling me funny stories about the silly things that happened at work.

It frightens me that each day my image of him grows slightly more blurry. It's as if I'm letting him die a second time by not keeping his memory vivid. My mother is no help. Whenever I try to discuss him, she gets this very forlorn expression on her face and changes the subject. I realize it's painful for her to talk about him. But in the long run, I think it would hurt less than bottling up her feelings the way she does. I wish I could say this to her, but I can't. Lately, she's been telling me how far away I seem to be a lot of the time. It's strange, but that's exactly the way I've always felt about her.

I know we're supposed to accept the inevitable and all that, but sometimes I can't help wondering how different my life would be if Papa was still alive; if the truck he was driving hadn't crashed that night. But whenever I start thinking about him, I get this terrible yearning. It's hard to explain. It's as if no matter what I do, I'll never be able to catch up with life. Because what I want most is already in the past and can't ever be recaptured. Whenever that feeling comes over me, I shut myself up in my room with my guitar and I try to write a song. It's the only thing that helps.

Chapter 5

When I enter the apartment, I find my mother standing by the sink chopping vegetables for dinner. She works quickly and efficiently, the way she does most things. Aunt Yolanda is nowhere in sight.

"I'm glad you're home, Alicia. I was beginning to get worried."

Despite the tired lines around her mouth, my mother is still a good looking woman. Relatives are always carrying on about how well she's kept her figure. "To look at you, you'd never think you turned forty last month," Aunt Yolanda commented recently. "To listen to you, that's another story," she added.

Aunt Yolanda likes to tease my mother about the fact that she's always acted a lot older than her age. My mother usually listens to it for a while. Then she'll draw herself up stiffly and say, "Better my way than a mature woman who still behaves like a teenager." But Yolanda just laughs.

Tonight, my mother seems to be in a pretty good mood. So instead of waiting to tell her about the Great Wave, I start right in. "Mama, you'll never guess what! The greatest thing just happened to me —" But before I can build any kind of momentum, she's cut me off.

"Calm down. I have some good news, too, for a change."

This is certainly a switch. "You do?"

"Yes," she replies with a funny little smile.

"I had a long talk about you with Mr. Miller, Junior," she explains.

Mr. Miller, Junior, is the son of Mr. Miller, Senior. Mr. Miller, Senior, is the founder and owner of Miller and Son, the sportswear factory where my mother is employed. About a year ago March, Mr. Miller, Senior had a pacemaker installed, and the following Labor Day, he officially retired, finally allowing Junior free rein. According to my mother, it's the best thing that ever happened to the firm. But Yolanda works there, too, and she doesn't seem to have noticed any change.

"Let me get this straight," I say. "You

and Mr. Miller, Junior, had a conversation about me?"

"That's right," Mama exclaims. I can't remember when I've seen her this excited. "I told him how you always get A's in math at John Adams. In geography, intermediate algebra, trigonometry, too."

I don't believe what I'm hearing.

"And then I explained how you had to take a special test to get into John Adams in the first place. But he already knew about the school. 'Yes,' he told me. 'I know they maintain the highest academic standards of any public school in the city.' "

I'm growing a little fidgety because I can't see where this conversation is going.

Mama continues, looking like the cat that ate the canary. "He's looking for an assistant bookkeeper for the summer. Someone to train for the future — and to keep on part-time in the fall. He said you sounded perfect for the job, so tomorrow he's going to give you an interview." So that's it. "And he's paying fifteen percent above minimum wage," she adds for good measure. I do some quick calculating and figure what that would come to for a thirty-five hour week. I'm no Einstein, but with all due modesty, math has always been a cinch for me. What it adds up to is not a bad salary for a mere sixteen-year-old, I find myself thinking.

All the time she's been talking, my mother has continued rhythmically chopping vegetables. "Today when I heard about the job, at first I was nervous to ask for you. But in this world, Alicia, sometimes you have to be a little pushy."

It's time to come clean. "Mama, I already have a job," I confess.

"Since when?" Now it's her turn to be puzzled.

"Since this afternoon." She stops chopping and looks at me warily.

I seize the opening and tell her about the afternoon's triumph. She listens but she looks irritated.

"I wish that Steve would stop filling your head with crazy ideas," she says the moment I pause for breath. "*He* can afford to take some silly job in a coffee shop."

"Coffee *house*," I protest pointlessly.

"Coffee shop, coffee house, it's all the same," she bristles. "A waste of your valuable time. You're not rich like Steve. You've got to think about your future, Alicia." The urgency in her voice jars me.

"I *am* thinking about my future. Lots of important people catch the shows at the Great Wave. Agents, producers, directors.

I could even get a record contract before the summer's over," I hear myself saying. Okay, so I'm stretching it a bit, but it *is* possible.

Just a few moments ago, Mama looked as excited as a little girl. Now her face has hardened. Before I know it, she's plopped a tomato into my hand. "Before you pack your bags for Hollywood, help me make dinner. You don't want to go there on an empty stomach."

Sometimes her sarcasm really gets on my nerves. This is one of those times. "Why is it so crazy to think I can make money as a singer?"

Instead of raising her voice, her tone only becomes cold. "I tell you what, Alicia. Next phone bill we get, instead of making out a money order, I'll send you down to the telephone company and you can sing them your songs. We'll see how far that gets us."

I throw the tomato down on the counter. It splatters all over the newly washed floor, but I'm too upset to care. "Daddy would have never said a thing like that," I shout. "He used to tell me I had a pretty voice." My eyes sting from holding back my tears. I manage to control myself until I've run to my room and slammed the door shut. Then I let go.

Why does Mama have to ruin everything for me? She could have at least congratulated me. But the only thing she knows how to do is put me down.

Before I can really work myself up, Mama has entered my room and approached me. "You do have a pretty voice, *niña*," she says gently. *Niña* is Spanish for little girl. It was her favorite name for me when I was a kid, but she hardly uses it any longer. "But a lot of other people have nice voices, too," she continues softly. "How many of them can make a living with their singing — maybe one in a hundred thousand." As she speaks, she sits on my bed and strokes my hair. "That's why I want you to think sensible. It hasn't been easy for us since your Papa died. What I make doesn't go very far."

Although I'm still angry, she looks so sad that my heart aches for her. "I know, Ma, I know." It's weird. But suddenly I feel as if I should be comforting her.

She lowers her voice even more, like she's about to make a big confession. "*Niña*, it was very hard for me to get the courage to talk to Mr. Miller today."

I can believe it. Mama's always been shy. I want to shout, it was hard for me to audition for Jessica Flynn. Only I don't.

"This is a big favor Mr. Miller is doing." To hear her tell it, you'd think he was offering a junior partnership in the firm. "When you graduate from high school next year, with no experience, you think it's going to be easy to find a good job? It's not. That's why tomorrow it's important you make a good impression. Nobody says you have to stay with Mr. Miller forever. But a better start than this, you're not going to find."

Already she's acting like it was settled. And what's worse, I don't murmur a word of protest. Don't panic, kid. You've only consented to go on an interview, I remind myself. It's called playing for time until you can come up with a counter strategy.

But then my mother tightens the noose. "So use your head, *niña*. Forget about this Great Wave," she croons as she continues to stroke my hair. Her voice has a lulling effect on me. Then she nestles me against her and I get a queasy sensation. It's like slipping into a trance, half against my will. But only half.

Just a few hours ago, all I could think of was the Great Wave. Now when I force myself to focus on today's audition, it's almost like recalling a mysterious event that occurred in a distant dream.

Chapter 6

"Alicia, hurry up," Mama calls to me from the kitchen. I don't know how she does it, but she always sounds wide awake at breakfast time. Somehow she manages to operate on full cylinders from the second her alarm clock goes off. Today, her voice sounds disgustingly cheerful. Unlike my mom, I'm generally a zombie when I first roll out of bed. This morning, I'm in a worse fog than usual because I'm dreading my nine o'clock appointment with Mr. Miller, Junior.

"You don't want to be late, Alicia," Mom shouts.

"I'm coming," I yell back as I tuck in my blouse. I'm wearing this 1940's style shirt I found in a thrift shop on St. Mark's Place. Usually the stuff you can pick up there is not so great unless you're a super shopper like Robin. The print is dynamite and splashy without being too campy and I really like the shoulder pads.

From my room I can smell the bacon and eggs my mother is cooking. In hygiene class last semester, I was the only student who could truthfully state I had eaten a protein breakfast every single morning of my life. Not that I'd had any choice in the matter. When I was in kindergarten, Mama read this article that listed all the terrible things that happen to kids who don't eat adequate breakfasts. They get fidgety; they can't concentrate on their school work; their bones don't develop. Basically, they're ruined for life. Ever since then, Mama's been convinced that any woman who allows her kid out of the house without first making sure she's eaten breakfast is an unfit parent.

I hear the click of high heels in the outside hallway. That means Aunt Yolanda has arrived. She drops by most weekday mornings. She and Mama ride the subway to work together. "It's even more beautiful out than yesterday," I hear her exclaim as she enters. "What a sin we have to be locked away in a factory all day." It's funny — even when my Aunt Yo is griping about something, she sounds more cheerful than most people do when they're not complaining.

By the time I've joined them in the kitchen, she's slipped off her shoes, settled herself at the breakfast table and is gulping down a cup of coffee. "I'll say one thing for your Mama, *querida*," she says as she greets me. "Of all the family, she makes the best coffee — good and strong."

"I'm glad I can do something right," Mama retorts. She is at the stove dishing out my bacon and eggs onto a plate. Her back is towards me.

"Your problem, Inez, is that you can't do anything wrong," Aunt Yo counters. It's not even eight A.M. but already they're off and running.

Then Yo abruptly switches the subject. "What a terrific time I had last night. That Tomás, he's a real romantic," she says.

"Just what you need," my mother frowns. She doesn't like it when her sister talks about her dates in front of me, even though everything Aunt Yo says is usually pretty harmless.

"You'll never guess where he took me," Yolanda continues. My mother's disapproval has never deterred her in the least. "Dancing on a ship in the moonlight," she tells us before we can reply. She looks almost radiant.

"No kidding." This Tomás sounds kind of promising. "On a luxury liner?" I ask. I imagine Aunt Yo on a deck illuminated by a hundred Japanese lanterns. She is twirling about in Tomás' arms to a Viennese waltz played by a thirty-piece orchestra.

"No, *mi amor*, not a luxury liner . . . the Staten Island Ferry." Aunt Yo's voice is a bit sheepish.

"I didn't know they had dancing on the ferry," I reply as casually as possible. I wouldn't want her to know I find the unglamorous truth a letdown.

"They don't," she confesses. "Tomás brought his radio."

My mother rolls her eyes.

"You should have seen how many people joined in," Yolanda says brightly. "Especially when the station played a mambo." Mama couldn't possibly look less impressed. But you've got to hand it to my aunt. She lets very little stand between her and a good time. When Steve said some were born to party, he must have had her in mind.

Mama frowns as she checks me out.

"When you finish your eggs, go change your blouse," she orders.

"What's wrong with what I have on?" I groan.

"You look like a hippie in it."

It's no use explaining I don't look anything like a hippie. There's even less point in telling her no one's used that term since I was in kindergarten.

Yolanda comes to my rescue — or tries to anyway. "Leave her alone, Inez. Alicia looks nice and lively in that blouse."

"Nice and lively isn't what a boss looks for in a bookkeeper," my mother snaps. "Wear your white blouse — the one with the Peter Pan collar," she says firmly.

Needless to say it's about the wimpiest thing I own. But I decide not to make a big deal over it. Losing a round doesn't matter, I remind myself. Winning the war is what counts. And if I want my mother to let me work at the Great Wave, giving her a rough time on small issues is not a good battle plan.

"You fuss over her too much," I overhear Aunt Yo saying while I'm in my room changing.

"I can't help it," Mama answers.

"Inez, it's been four years since Francisco died. Isn't it time you worried about yourself for a change?" Yo suggests. "Go out, have some fun."

Aunt Yo has said this to my mother roughly a hundred times. It always falls on deaf ears, but that doesn't discourage a trooper like my aunt.

My white blouse just sort of hangs on me. I scramble through my drawers for a scarf. That way, once the interview is over and I check in at school, I can jazz myself up a little.

"I tell you what, Inez," my aunt continues. "Tomás has this friend, Diego. Diego Santiago. A little on the short side maybe, but what a sense of humor. He always keeps me in stitches."

"Everybody keeps you in stitches." What's fair is fair. My mother has a point. I've even seen Aunt Yo chuckle at the weather report.

"But this Diego is so funny," she persists. "I bet he even makes *you* laugh." Now that would really be something. If this Diego managed to get two solid belly laughs from Mama, he probably should think seriously about pursuing a career as a stand-up comic.

While I'm killing time choosing a pair of earrings to wear, Aunt Yolanda proposes that the four of them get together some night.

"What for?" My mother's voice is flat and expressionless. "So we can do the mambo on the Staten Island Ferry maybe? You want to make a fool of yourself at your age, that's your business, Yolanda. But don't expect me to keep you company." Dead silence follows these words. Aunt Yo may be good natured and all, but I'm afraid this time Mama has gone too far.

"Alicia, what's taking you so long?" she calls to me. Her voice sounds impatient. I realize I've held off as long as possible and go to join them.

Mrs. Reuben greets us as we exit from the building. A few seconds ago, my mother was eager to get going, but now she stops to chat. "Alicia is going for a job interview — in an office," she informs Mrs. Reuben proudly. Honestly, from her tone you'd think she had said Oval Office.

"Good luck, Alicia," Mrs. Reuben says. But if you ask me, she looks sort of dubious. "I used to go to business, too," she continues. "Same company, thirty-seven years. In all that time, I took only fifteen days sick leave." Although this isn't exactly new information, I suddenly feel my stomach muscles tightening. "When I retired, the company gave me a plaque," she adds modestly.

"Congratulations," Mama answers.

"With a record like that, they should have given you stock in the company," Yolanda jokes.

"From your mouth to God's ears," Mrs. Reuben says wistfully. She seems so frail it's hard to imagine her as the picture of health when she was young. I told Steve about her work record once and he gasped in horror. "Even felons get more time off for good behavior," he pointed out. I laughed at the time. Right now his remark doesn't seem funny.

Miller and Son is located in the upper twenties, only a few short subway stops away. I hadn't been there in ages, so it was a surprise to discover that the brick exterior had been newly washed and the woodwork had been freshly painted. In comparison, the other buildings on the street looked grimier than ever. Sprucing up the exterior was one of Miller Junior's first improvements, Mama says as we reach the site. As further proof, she points to the fancy new sign, which says *Miller and Son: Fashion Sportswear.*

"Now if only he would fix up the inside," Aunt Yolanda sighs. This reminds me that in all the years my mother has worked there, I've never actually been inside. Whenever I'd meet her after work, she always insisted that I wait for her outside on the sidewalk, even in the dead of winter. This morning she directs me towards the small lobby where I can catch an elevator up to the front office. It's a separate entrance from the one leading to the factory section. "Get off at the third floor and tell the receptionist you have an appointment with Mr. Miller," she instructs me.

Her co-workers stream past us into the factory. In a few moments she and Aunt Yo will have to join them. So far she hasn't lectured me on the importance of making a knockout impression on Junior. But now I can tell it's coming. She places a hand firmly on my shoulder and looks at me straight in the eye. I brace myself. But all she says is, "I know I can trust you to do your best, Alicia." That's it. Period. What's more, her tone is real low-keyed. Before I realize it, I'm nodding solemnly. Once again, Inez Marin has succeeded in throwing me off balance.

As I glance up, I notice Aunt Yolanda winking at me. It's as if she's saying, lighten up, it's only a crummy job interview — and for a job I don't even want! All the same, it comes as no real surprise that by the time I've pressed the elevator button, I'm hoping that I won't let Mama down by making a fool of myself in front of Junior. That's what a pro she is at turning the screws on me.

Chapter 7

"So tell me, Ms. Marin, how long have you had this burning desire to become a book-keeper?" Junior asks as his lead-off question.

"I've always enjoyed working with figures." Not a memorable answer, I'm afraid, and to make matters worse, my voice lacks conviction.

"Your mother told me that math is one of your best subjects at school," he says earnestly.

A phone call interrupts us. "Sorry, Harry, Monday is too late. I need that wool by Thursday," Mr. Miller informs his caller as he leans back in his swivel chair. He still sounds genial, but if I were Harry, I wouldn't press my luck.

After he hangs up, Junior compliments me on the high scores I got on the tests I had taken before I was admitted to his office. First, a personality test designed to root out hardcore psychos. Once his secretary was sure I wouldn't set the building on fire, she moved on to arithmetic and English usage. The math I could do in my sleep; the English wasn't exactly challenging.

"Well, so far, so good," Junior comments as he quickly flips through my test scores. "You've rounded second base. But to reach home plate, you've got to meet our Senior Bookkeeper, Mrs. Kvares." This corny baseball lingo is really making me wonder.

"Mrs. Kvares likes to throw her weight around a bit," he says as he leads me down the hall to her office. "But inside, she's all heart. It's just that she's worked for the firm for so long, she's convinced she can run it better than I do," he continues in this real confidential manner, like he trusts me enough to let me in on a company secret. "Who's to say, maybe she could," he shrugs and smiles good-naturedly.

I smile back, politely I hope.

To my relief, I immediately like Mrs. Kvares. She is about fifty, large boned and has a pair of lungs that won't quit. I bet even when she whispers it carries to the second balcony. She strikes me as someone who'll always let you know exactly where you stand with her. Maybe that's why I feel comfortable. In the long run, you lose less sleep hanging out with straight shooters.

When she starts rattling off the assistant bookkeeper's job duties, I spring to attention pronto. The factory payroll is the major responsibility, from what she says. At first it sounds pretty complicated: The operators get paid for the number of garments they complete. There is no set fee. They get paid one price for skirts, another for camisoles, a third for long-sleeved blouses and so forth. And after I figure out what an operator has earned in a particular week, I have to compute her individual tax deductions.

"It's not hard once you get the hang of it," she assures me. "Tedious, that's another story." She sighs.

She throws me a few sample questions. Luckily, I manage to come up with the correct answers without any embarassingly long pauses. "It's nice to have a live one around for a change," she tells Junior. She sounds almost impressed! But before I can develop a swelled head, she puts the whole thing in perspective.

"I won't tell you what he's been trying to palm off on me," she groans. Miller the Younger squirms a little. "The daughter of his doubles partner in tennis — the niece of his broker! From the latest styles, they knew. From adding and subtracting, we won't go into it," she continues.

"Come on, Dorrie. So I tried to do a couple of friends a favor," Miller finally cuts her off. "What's the big deal?" He is mildly annoyed, but this doesn't faze her in the least.

"They wouldn't have stayed friends for long. Not once you saw what those girls would have done to your payroll," she informs him. This takes the wind out of his sails, at least momentarily.

It's later that afternoon and Steve and I are hanging out on the roof of my building. Steve is pacing up and down, close to the roof's edge. I've just told him about Mr. Miller's use of baseball terminology, which bordered on the obsessive. "Stop putting me on, Marin. He didn't really talk like that," Steve says.

"It was like once he started, he couldn't stop," I explain. According to Miller the Younger, the other applicants "struck out."

I, on the other hand, had "fielded all of Mrs. Kvares' curve balls." So he was "confident I'd end the season with a high batting average." As I talk I realize what really upset me was the way I let myself get carried away by the momentum of the situation. Instead of sorting out my real feelings, I just cheerfully agreed to everything. Take the way I had jumped to thank Junior when he told me I'd been hired. What's more, I had sounded pleased, even grateful.

The sun is beating down on us. I'm beginning to feel more and more out of it. Less than twenty-four hours ago, I was just another statistic on the teenage unemployment rolls. Now I have one job more than I know what to do with.

Steve is still pacing. He loves hanging out on my roof. If a New York City kid can't get away during the summer, he considers a rooftop the next best thing. In my neighborhood, we call it going to Tar Beach. I even wrote a song with that title once. It was about this spunky woman who refuses to be brought down by the fact that she's stuck in the sweltering city all summer. It was inspired by my Aunt Yolanda.

"Why did you have to score so high on the math part?" Steve asks reproachfully. He definitely does not share my aptitude for math, and the idea of someone spending seven hours daily computing a company payroll strikes him as cruel and unusual punishment.

He stops pacing and shakes his head sadly. "At the very least, Marin, couldn't you have cracked bubble gum during the interview?"

"I couldn't mess up on purpose."

Steve smirks. "No, of course not. Not an overachiever like you."

"My mother would have brained me, numbskull." I'd already told him how happy she was when we met outside at lunchtime and I'd told her the news. You'd think we had won the jackpot on *Family Feud.* "Besides, I can live with being Mrs. Kvares' assistant for one summer. The bookkeeping job isn't the bummer. It's having to give up singing at the Great Wave."

"When did you decide you didn't mind the bookkeeping gig?"

"When I thought about the money we need."

"Then do both jobs," he shrugs.

"Huh?"

"You heard me. Work both jobs. The hours don't conflict." The solution is so simple, it's boring him. "I mean you *are* disgustingly healthy, Marin. You'll hold up for the summer."

"Thanks." For a remark intended to be encouraging, it sure sounds like a swipe.

"There's only one hitch," I remind him.

"What's that?"

"My mother. . . . She'll never let me work both jobs . . ." My voice trails off.

Steve makes no effort to conceal his irritation. "You'll never know for sure until you ask her. Just appeal to her rationally."

I have to laugh. "That may work fine with your parents. *My* mother hasn't spent six years on a shrink's couch," I remind him. "Rational approaches don't work with her." The minute these words are out of my mouth, I realize they're a low blow and regret them.

But Steve just grins. "It's worth a try, Marin," he continues after a beat. His eyes glint mischievously. "There must be something Grandmother Esperanza said you can turn to for inspiration." He improvises. "Like 'There is no nut so tough that it cannot be cracked.' Isn't that the saying that clinched her title of the Ben Franklin of the *barrio*?" he deadpans.

I have to hand it to Steve. No matter how low a blow I've dealt him, he can always be counted on to stoop even lower — without flinching, either.

Chapter 8

I'm flipping the *pasteles* in the pan when I hear the doorknob turn. My mother is home already. I tense. Then I remind myself of the advice Steve gave me once we settled down in earnest to work out a strategy. The gist of it was, "No matter how your mother carries on, you keep your cool."

"I felt like making *pasteles*," I tell Mama as she enters the kitchen. They're these meat and pastry patties she likes a lot. I don't get domestic urges too often so I hope my voice sounds casual. I wouldn't want to tip my hand. "Oh, and I remembered to pick up your sandals at the shoemaker," I add.

At first she doesn't answer. She carefully takes in the neatly set table. When she turns towards me, she has this real sarcastic expression on her face. It's the look she gets when Aunt Yo tries to talk her into something she's dead set against. Then she comes straight to the point. "Alicia, *mi amor*, whatever you got up your sleeve, it's not going to work. You should be happy they gave you the bookkeeping job, instead of trying to wriggle out of it." My mother was never one to waste much time on preliminaries.

"I'm not trying to wriggle out of it," I protest. "But I do have a plan I'd like to discuss."

"Forget about it," she tells me through clenched teeth.

"Just listen!" I plead. She sighs and sits down.

I take a deep breath and launch into the speech I had rehearsed with Steve earlier. "A — the bookkeeping job is from nine to five, Monday through Friday." So far so good. "B — the coffee house hours are from six to eleven, Tuesdays through Saturdays."

That's as far as I get. "C — the answer is no," she snaps.

"Why not, Mama?" I wail. So much for keeping cool. "I can work both jobs," I insist.

"It's too much. You'll be tired all the time."

"No, I won't. It's only a fifty-five hour work week total. Years ago, people used to work longer hours than that."

"They used to die younger, too."

"It's only for the summer, Mama. Besides working at the coffee house isn't really a job."

"And what is it, then?" she asks.

"More like fun," I try to explain.

"Yes, lots of fun," she scoffs. "Standing on your feet for hours, taking people's orders like a servant with the men saying fresh things to you. So you get to sing a song once in a while." She shrugs. "The way you make it sound, it's like you should pay them for the privilege."

She really *doesn't* understand, I realize. Most people would never dream of getting up and singing in front of an audience. But that's because they can't carry a tune or are too scared. With Mama, it's more like she's not even tempted. She can't even understand how I could find the idea appealing. It's times like these that I miss Papa the most. Since appealing to her on artistic grounds is getting me nowhere fast, I switch to arguments that are more up her alley. "With the money I make at the coffee house, I'll be able to cover all my expenses next term. My clothes, everything," I add. "And that means you can keep all of my bookkeeping salary."

She shakes her head. "That's very nice, *niña*, but it's just not a good idea."

At least she called me *niña*. That's a sign she's softening. I press my case. I know she's behind on bills, I tell her. Then I run down all the household things she's wanted to buy but couldn't afford — like new couch covers and fancy pots from Macy's department store. Finally I tell her that if I work both jobs, we'd save enough for her to go to San Juan for a week. Grandmother Esperanza's health hasn't been good. Although she doesn't talk about it much, I know Mama is worried she won't get to see her again before she dies.

My mother admits the extra money will come in handy, but in the long run, it's more important for me not to blow the opportunity Mr. Miller is offering me. "Alicia, it could lead to something," she persists.

"Yeah — more of the same," I mutter under my breath. "Mama, I swear I won't mess up at the office," I say.

"Not on purpose, maybe. But, *niña*, when

a person tries to do too much, they end up doing nothing right," she answers.

However, she finally agrees to give my plan a trial run. Naturally, she has a hundred and one conditions. Steve has to see me home every night. Luckily, that's no problem, since he already offered to. Next, I have to be home by midnight at the latest. And under no circumstances am I to give any of the male customers I serve my home phone number or any other personal information.

"It'll work out, Mama. Don't worry," I try to assure her as I dish out the *pasteles* and the salad. In the excitement, I'd almost forgotten about dinner. As we sit down to eat, my mother unfolds her napkin in her lap. I get a kick out of watching her. It's only paper, but from the way she handles it, you'd think it was fancy linen, and she was a society lady about to eat the first course of a lavish banquet in some swanky hotel. You'd never guess she was sitting down at our chipped formica table in our tiny kitchen, eating my overcooked *pasteles*.

"I know I can handle both jobs," I add for good measure once she's taken a bite of her *pastel* and seems to like it.

She sighs wearily and shakes her head. "You don't know what it's like to handle one job. So of course you think you can handle two."

"I won, I won." I squeal. It's after dinner and I'm calling Steve from the pay phone at Raoul's candy store around the corner. Talking on the phone at home is impossible when my mother is around. The phone in our apartment is located smack on the kitchen wall — not exactly great for privacy. What's more, my mother gets freaked out if we rack up so much as a couple of extra message units on our monthly bill. So either I wait for my friends to call me and then respond mostly in monosyllables, or when something major comes up, I rush out to Raoul's with a handful of nickels.

Considering the time Steve had put in coaching me, I figured the least I could do was give him a progress report. As expected, he is really happy that my mother gave in. Naturally he can't refrain from saying, "I told you so," but I guess he's entitled.

The next day at school, I spring it on Robin that I snagged a gig at the Great Wave. Generally, Robin makes it an iron-clad rule to display as little emotion as possible. This time, though, she seems genuinely excited. Impressed, even. Steve, in particular, is surprised by this unexpected display. Robin's super cool attitude has always driven him up the wall. He's always making dumb digs like "Your expressions run the gamut from bland to bored." Or, "What do you plan to call your memoirs — *Born Blasé?*" Stuff like that. He thinks these cracks are funny. But he's never succeeded in getting a rise out of Robin with any of them. Mostly she stonewalls him; now and then, she'll go as far as to stifle a yawn.

She once expressed her philosophy to me. "I have feelings like everyone else," she said. "I just think it's tacky to gush."

Today, however, between spoonfuls of yogurt, she keeps repeating how disappointed she is that she won't be around to witness my professional debut. The moment school ends, Robin is scheduled to leave for summer camp. If she doesn't seem too excited at the prospect, it's because she's gone to this same camp in New Hampshire forever. Her mother had gone there, too, when she was a girl. "I guess you could call it a family tradition," Robin said nonchalantly when she first told me about it. My hunch is that Robin does her casual routine so that I won't feel deprived. My mother could never afford to send me to camp, so Robin pretends it's all a big drag. As blunt as she can be about some things, Robin is very sensitive in other areas. Last summer, she sent me tons of postcards giving me the weekly highlights — or "lowlights" as she calls them. "It's hard to believe, but the current Head Counselor is even nerdier than last year's." Or "I've run through three cans of insect repellent in one week." Or "The boys can live without me, but the mosquitos sure can't."

But no matter how grim Robin tried to make it sound, the truth is her postcards only made me wish I could be in New Hampshire, too. Let's face it, it sure beats hanging out on Tar Beach. It suddenly hits me that now I won't feel that way. Thanks to Jessica hiring me at the Great Wave, I wouldn't trade places with Robin for anything in the world.

Chapter 9

"Last year, when they were renovating, Sonny offered me a larger space," Mrs. Kvares is telling me. (That's her nickname for Junior.) "Instead I opted for a smaller office and a big window." It's my first day as an employee of Miller and Son, and Mrs. Kvares is giving me the lay of the land.

"Nobody is going to drop dead from the view, but sunlight is sunlight," she points out. I couldn't agree more. Few things depress me as much as dark, airless places.

The office may be small but it's as cheerful as the Henry Street daycare center I used to go to when I was little. Lots of leafy plants in bright plastic pots. Exotic travel posters of places like Rio de Janeiro and Thailand on the walls. Plus dozens of snapshots of Mrs. Kvares' children and grandchildren all over the place. The biggest photo is one of her husband wearing a huge sombrero.

"I know he looks goofy, but I still get a kick out of it," she says when she notices me glancing at it. "It was taken on a trip to Acapulco. First real vacation I talked him into taking in eleven years. Usually we just spend two weeks in the Catskills." She sighs. The Catskills are a mountain resort area in upstate New York. I've never been there but I had heard a little about it from Papa. His band played a couple of gigs there one summer.

To tell the truth, I'm surprised at how chatty Mrs. Kvares is being. I thought she wouldn't have wasted a minute before getting down to basics. Shows you how wrong I can be. After insisting I eat the other half of her toasted bagel, she finally gets around to filling me in on the details of the job.

In between, though, she continues to talk a blue streak — telling me how much she loves to travel, and griping about her youngest son, David. David Kvares, according to his mother, is not a bad kid. But he's a little short on get up and go. Pushing twenty-six (that's a kid?) and still working in a greenhouse on Long Island, Mrs. Kvares laments. I don't know what to tell her. It doesn't sound like a bad job to me, I mean, if that's what he likes.

Actually, I don't mind Mrs. Kvares talking so much. I've always had a soft spot in my heart for big gabbers, especially when Mama is so quiet. Mama makes me nervous sometimes. It's not because she's just being quiet. It's because I know that inside the wheels are clicking away, but she's keeping the full story to herself.

Take this morning, for example. We had arrived at work and were about to split for our separate entrances when I asked her where we should meet at lunch time. "Eat your sandwich in the bookkeeping office," she answered quickly. I was a little surprised. I had taken it for granted that we would get together during our lunch break. But when I started to press her about it, her eyes clouded over. "It's just not a good idea for you to come to the factory area" was the only comment I could coax out of her.

I decided to drop it. After all, I had other things on my mind at the moment. Mainly, whether I would be able to cut it as Assistant Bookkeeper. By the time five o'clock rolls around, I'm breathing easier on that score. Unless I'm kidding myself, I don't think the job will tax my brain cells beyond their capacity. Don't get me wrong. I'm not going to wake up each morning singing, "Yippee. Today I get to make out Miller, Junior's payroll." On the other hand, it's not going to be seven straight hours of torture.

The real test comes on Thursday. That's the first night I have to report to the Great Wave. Strange as it seems, it's not the prospect of having to get up and sing to a roomful of strangers that's making me uptight. What's really making me nervous is wondering whether I'll be able to carry a full tray overhand, waitress-style. Not just manage it, but somehow maneuver it through the kitchen's swinging doors and look breezy while I'm doing it.

"I hear you've become a full-fledged member of the labor force, Alicia," Mr. Lewis remarks as he passes me the sautéed broccoli. It's Wednesday evening and I'm eating dinner at Steve's house.

"Yeah, only sixteen and already slaving away in a humid sweatshop," Steve shakes his head sadly.

"My job is clerical, and the office is air conditioned," I feel compelled to point out. I don't want his parents to feel sorry for me.

"Ex – cuse me," Steve says, laying on the sarcasm even more thickly than usual.

"We're used to Steve's dramatizing everything," Mrs. Lewis assures me "Not every work situation is out of Dickens, darling," she comments to her son. It's easy to see where Steve gets his sense of humor. He could learn a thing or two from his mother's delivery, though. She definitely has a lighter touch.

"How come you married such a smart aleck, Art?" Steve asks his father. "I thought men of your generation made it a point to steer clear of women who gave them a lot of lip," he continues.

"He married me because he found me irresistible," Mrs. Lewis says matter-of-factly.

"Is that so, Art?" Steve teases.

"She was the only woman I'd ever met who laughed at my jokes." Mr. Lewis shrugs genially.

"I was the only woman who got them." I notice Mrs. Lewis giving her husband a private little wink. Considering how long they've been married, I think it's kind of neat the way they still flirt with one another.

"I could see where that would turn your head, Arthur," Steve concedes.

It kills me the way he calls his parents by their first names. Especially since he makes such a point of calling me by my last. "They like it that way, Marin," he claims. "It makes them feel young."

Steve's sister Danielle is seated opposite me. She is nine years old, and has a heart-shaped face and huge green eyes with heavy black-fringed lashes. Everything about her is dainty, from her voice to the way she eats her dinner in neat little bites. Steve always calls her The Knock-Out.

"Hey, how about passing me some more rice, Knock-Out?" he asks.

Without a murmur, Danielle picks up the platter and hands it to him. She always pretends to take his nickname for her in stride, but it's not hard to see that she's secretly pleased by it.

"The food is delicious, Mrs. Lewis," I comment.

"Oh, Art deserves the credit, not me," she corrects me with a pleased smile.

"It's just something I threw together in our new wok," Mr. Lewis says modestly. But it's obvious he's lapping up the praise.

"My husband took a course in Szechuan cooking last fall," Mrs. Lewis explains proudly.

"I enrolled on a whim. To my surprise, I discovered I had a real flair for it," he adds sort of shyly.

Steve snorts. "If the Yang Sun Inn had an opening for a chef, Art would probably give up his law practice."

His mother arches her eyebrows. "Does it embarrass you to have a father who cooks for his family?" she challenges her son. She knows Steve would never admit to holding such a macho attitude.

"No, but let's face it, Ellie," Steve retorts. "It's a real status symbol."

"What is?" She is beginning to sound vaguely annoyed.

"Being the first woman in your N.O.W. chapter whose husband knows his way around a wok," he replies.

Mrs. Lewis frowns. Mr. Lewis goes on the offense and abruptly changes the subject. "What did *Son of Poltergeist* gross in Buffalo last week?" he asks.

Steve ignores his father's remark and concentrates on chewing the large shrimp he's popped into his mouth.

Mr. Lewis refuses to take the hint. "Is it true Elvis Costello broke the box office record at Caesar's Palace this spring?" he persists.

Steve groans. I guess it can be a drag to have parents who think it's cool to make fun of rock stars.

"Don't look so put upon," Mrs. Lewis admonishes her son. "Your father was only kidding."

"No, he wasn't," Steve blurts out. "Art is terrified I'll disgrace him when I grow up."

"How's that?" Mr. Lewis asks mildly.

"For heaven's sake, Steve, where did you ever get such an outlandish notion?" his mother asks.

"It's not outlandish." Steve is genuinely upset. " 'Fess up, Art. You're worried I'll become an agent with the William Morris Agency or something."

Mr. Lewis draws a blank. "It never crossed my mind," he says when he recovers his voice. "But now that you've mentioned it, the thought is enough to make me break out in a cold sweat."

Steve's often tried to tell me that his parents aren't nearly as supportive of him as I think. Until tonight, I didn't understand what he meant. Their style may be a lot different than my mother's, but they still manage to make their disapproval clear.

After dinner, in between playing his

latest albums for me, Steve blows off steam. "It's okay with them if I go into the arts," he explains. "As long as I do something they consider classy — like playing the violin in a string quartet or becoming an expert on modern Scandinavian poetry. As long as it's an area where there's no prayer I'll ever earn a buck," he adds bitterly. "I guess you could consider that their main criteria."

It's funny about parents. They all have definite ideas about what they'd like their kids to do with their lives. Or at least they know what they *don't* want them to do. But it seems to me that their ambitions usually have a lot more to do with their own goals than with their children's interests. As for whether their kids would be happy leading the lives they've planned for them, sometimes I don't think that thought ever crosses their minds.

Chapter 10

It's my first night at the Great Wave. To my relief, waiting on tables hasn't been the bummer I expected it to be. After Larry, the manager, told me I didn't have to carry trays overhand, I was able to breathe more easily. To be honest, you couldn't exactly call Larry a demanding supervisor. His two main instructions were, "Don't yawn in anyone's face while you're taking his order," and "If you're afraid you're about to spill something, try to aim *away* from the customer's clothing."

"How are your feet holding up?" Steve checks in with me as I carry a couple of cappucinos to one of my tables.

"My feet are fine. When do I get to sing?" I can't believe how pushy I'm acting. On the other hand, it *is* getting late, and the last thing I need is Mama on my back for not coming in on time.

"Don't worry," Steve answers. I remind him of my curfew. He nods. Before he returns to his podium, I notice him saying a few words to Jessica.

It's funny. If I'd been scheduled to lead off the first set, I probably would have begged for a later slot. But waiting on tables for a few hours while my fellow waiters and waitresses each had a crack at the limelight has magically cured my stage fright. I can think of only one thing worse than bombing out in front of an audience — and that's not getting the chance to bomb out!

Before I know it, Jessica has come to tell me that I'm on next. I'm really grateful for the casual way she wishes me good luck. Somehow, I manage to get rid of my tray and apron and get on stage with my guitar in hand as soon as Steve finishes his introduction. What's more, my knees aren't even buckling with fear. In fact, you could even go so far as to call me confident. Otherwise, I doubt I'd pick *The Great American Hit* as my opening number. That's the song where I let it all hang out — where I come clean about my fantasy life. It's all there. My dreams of making the Top Ten charts and of being interviewed by *Rolling Stone*, not to mention the crowds lining the streets of old San Juan when I visit there.

> "In your heart of hearts you feel
>   you'll be a star,
> And tonight, at home alone,
>   that's what you are.
> 'Cause your mirror promises
>   that you've got what it takes,
> The only thing you're missing
>   is the breaks."

Right away, I sense I'm clicking. And nothing opens me up more than the feeling that I've grabbed the audience's attention.

> "And you could write the Great
>   American Hit,
> You could write the next Great
>   American Hit.
> Oh yeah, tonight, somewhere,
>   someone out there
> Could be singin' it,
> Singin' it. . . ."

Knock on wood. The crowd's still with me. No one's thrown a tomato at me, or coughed or even rattled a saucer. But even though I realize I'm going over okay, I'm still surprised at the amount of applause I get when I finish. Don't get me wrong. The crowd hasn't jumped to their feet and stamped them wildly. But it's a safe bet to say they enjoyed themselves.

Next I sing a ballad about my second cousin Carlos. It's about how he started taking junk at twelve and spent most of his teens in and out of addiction centers. I guess you could call the song downbeat. But I don't think it's morbid or anything. To me, it's really about the power of hope. Because no matter how many times he's slipped, Carlos still believes that someday he'll kick his habit for good. To hear him talk about it, you'd never think that maybe he's just kidding himself. That's how convincing he sounds.

This time the audience claps even louder. Performing can really be something else — especially when you're singing your own material. I mean, just a few moments ago I was waiting on some of the people I am now entertaining. Most of them were pretty friendly. Yet I never felt for a second that we were anything but total strangers. It's basically the same barrier I feel with most people. When you come right down to it, how often does anyone move beyond the "Hi, how ya doing?" stage? If you're me, the answer is, "not very often."

When I'm alone on stage, with the lights blurring the audience's faces, you'd think I'd feel an even greater barrier. Instead, the opposite is true. That's what I realized tonight. Reaching an audience means establishing an instant connection with them. For those few moments, you trust one another enough to let down your guard and share all your secrets. But then the curtain falls, and you go back to the same "Hi, how ya doing?" routine.

As far as my mother is concerned, the curtain didn't fall soon enough. It's past one by the time I tiptoe into the dark apartment. She startles me by flicking on the living room light. I realize I am in serious trouble.

You can chalk up my poor judgment to a couple of things. Holding an audience's attention can give you the illusion that you're also holding time in your hands — somehow making it stand still. And I have to admit that I got carried away by my reception. In addition to getting heavy applause, I had Steve raving about how well I did, and Larry and a few of the other performers offering their congratulations. Even Jessica went out of her way to tell me she'd been pleased. Considering the evening was easily the high point of my life, it's understandable that a routine thing like a curfew no longer seemed like such a big deal. But the minute I see my mother's stony stare, I know I've made a big mistake.

"So this is the way you keep your promise to me," she says. Her voice is icily calm.

"I'm sorry, Mama," I began. Then I immediately become flustered and start blabbing away about how there'd been a mix-up and I'd gone on later than I expected to, but that since the audience liked me, Jessica kept signalling to me to sing more songs. All of this happens to be true, but the frantic way I relay it would be enough to make anyone suspicious.

"The audience really liked me, Mama," I repeat lamely. I guess I need to convince her of that. But when her only reaction is to stare at me skeptically, doubts begin to creep in. Maybe I *am* overstating the public's reaction.

"So because they like you, that makes it all right to stay out half the night?" she finally comments, never shifting her piercing gaze from me for one second.

"Jessica promised to schedule me earlier

from now on. Honest, it won't happen again, I swear." I can't believe how flustered I'm acting. But then, my head-on collisions with my mother have always made me squirm. That's why I've avoided them whenever possible. So I don't understand why I should be surprised that I'm cringing. Unless it's because until I'd walked in that door, I felt that for once in my life, I had it all licked.

"Mr. Miller, maybe he doesn't give you applause," Mama continues, her anger erupting through her controlled surface. "But he gives you something better — a good paycheck every week. Only there's one catch." She's practically spitting out the words. I brace myself for the rest of them. "You have to be awake to earn it," she snaps. To my surprise, she doesn't go on. For the first time since I've entered, I notice how drained and worn she looks.

"I'll be awake tomorrow, don't worry," I promise timidly.

"We'll see." She frowns warily. "But I tell you right now, Alicia," she warns. Her voice is quiet, but I know she means business. "Come in late one more time and you can forget about the coffee house for good."

That idea is too awful to even contemplate. This is one occasion I'm not going to allow her to spoil, I decide. I mumble one more apology. Then I beat a hasty retreat to my room.

Although it's been a very long day, I'm too wound up to drop off to sleep right away. I recall my bus ride home with Steve, and how I kept badgering him over and over for reassurance. "Level with me," I pleaded. "Would you come back to hear me sing if you didn't know me?"

"Especially if I didn't know you," he retorted. "Because then I wouldn't have to be subjected to an inquisition. I hope this isn't a preview of what you'll put me through after your first major concert."

When I finally fall asleep, I dream I'm performing in a small but elegant club. My voice is rich and smooth as velvet, and I'm carrying off these complicated chord arrangements without a hitch. The song I'm singing has a haunting melody. The entire audience is attentive, but I am drawn toward one person in particular — a man seated alone at a side table near the front. Beyond the fact that I can see he's smiling, I can't make out his features. Yet I know I've seen him before. His presence is soothing. As long as he is there, I'm confident I'll have enough breath to sustain all the long notes and I'll be able to zip right through the complicated passages.

But I'm afraid to end my song, afraid if I stop singing even for a second that he will vanish — and my luck will vanish with him. So I keep on singing, and with each new verse, I gradually accelerate the tempo. Soon the song's pace has become frantic. But the man seems unaware that I am losing control. He continues to observe me calmly, a mysterious smile on his face.

I'm growing pretty exhausted when the stage lights shift slightly. Now I can see the man clearly for the first time. I gasp, it's Papa. As our eyes meet, I can even see the tiny yellow specks in his hazel pupils. Then his smile broadens. It's as if he's reassuring me that I've been doing just fine, but as I make a move toward him, his features once again grow indistinct. And the closer I move, the blurrier he becomes. I start to panic. My voice grows harsh. I'm singing off-key. Suddenly garish strobe lights begin flashing. I can't even tell if Papa is still in the room. Only a little while ago, I had the situation under control. Now I feel like I'm moving down an assembly line. Unless I jump off very soon, I'm going to disappear down a dark chute, but the line is moving too fast for me to jump off. My voice has become as shrill as a factory whistle. I know it's only a matter of moments before the audience will start booing me.

"Alicia, Alicia," I hear my mother call. She sounds exasperated. Dimly I make out her shadowy figure as she stands over my bed. In her hands she holds my alarm clock. "For ten minutes, your alarm has been ringing," she informs me. "In the middle of my bath I hear it." She shakes her head impatiently. "I hope it's not going to be like this every morning," she says as her parting shot.

I throw off my bed sheet and stumble groggily to the bathroom. But even after I splash tons of cold water on my face, I still have a hard time revving myself up to face the day. That moment in my dream when Papa and I suddenly locked eyes and I first recognized him keeps coming back to haunt me.

Chapter 11

By the time August rolls around, I've lost track of how often my mother has had to hover over me in the early morning, alarm clock in hand. Naturally, she's kept count of all the times I've dozed through the ringing alarm and she never misses a chance to remind me.

Not long after I started juggling both jobs, Steve ambled over to me as I was setting up my station at the Great Wave. He had a confession to make, he said. "From the looks of you, Marin, I've clearly overestimated how disgustingly healthy you are." I let him off the hook gracefully. "Any real woman would much rather be thought of as pale and interesting," I kid around. At least I think that's how a real woman would feel.

"Pale and frazzled would be a lot more

accurate in your case," Steve replies.

"Creep," I say genially as I stagger out to the kitchen to refill my sugar bowls.

There's no getting around it. Slaving over Junior's payroll seven hours daily, then rushing uptown to wait on tables has not been a breeze. On a few hectic nights, I even found myself violating Larry's number one rule. I yawned in a couple of customer's faces while I was taking their orders.

But getting the chance to perform at the Great Wave has been worth all the hassle. And no matter how exhausted I felt before I hit the stage, once I was on I had energy to spare.

It's amazing how much I've learned in four short weeks. Steve agrees. I now pace myself better; I've relaxed enough to realize I don't have to push all the time; I allow myself more quiet moments. I'm starting to trust that those moments can be just as effective as pulling out all the stops.

"How's it going, *querida*?" Yolanda wants to know. It's Monday, my night off. I'm on the couch staring at the TV in a semi-stupor. I'm too lost in my own thoughts to pay any attention to the show, yet too lazy to get up and flick it off.

"Oh fine, Aunt Yo," I chirp. Then the truth pours out. If only there were twice as many hours in the day, if only I didn't have to deal with rush hour traffic on route from my day job to my night gig. If only I didn't have to hold down a day job in the first place, I moan.

"If only you were Princess Di," Aunt Yo sighs in mock sympathy.

"If Alicia were Princess Di, she'd always have to wear a hat and gloves," my mother says as she joins us from the kitchen.

I decide to play along. "Gee, I never thought of that!" I exclaim. "Poor old Di. Next Command Performance I give, I'll have to remember to give her my sympathy."

Yolanda chuckles. "You know, you and your mother are more alike than you think," she observes. This is news to me. From the look on her face, this also comes as a surprise to my mother. But she chooses to ignore her sister's remark. Instead she says, "Lady Alicia, in case you forgot, you got a Command Performance with Miller and Son early tomorrow."

I take her hint and go to bed.

Tuesday morning I wake up without any problem. But Wednesday is a different story. Ditto, Thursday. Friday I hit a new low. Not only do I sleep right through the alarm, but the moment Mama finishes issuing her person-to-person wake up call, I collapse back in bed and doze off again.

When she finally does coax me out of bed, I reach into my bureau drawer and pull out the first t-shirt within my grasp. The mornings when I'd debate ten minutes over which scarf to wear are a thing of the past. These days I'm satisfied to leave the house wearing matching socks.

I drag myself to the kitchen table, slosh milk over my cereal, and take a few bites. "I'm glad the office is air-conditioned. It's supposed to be a real scorcher today," I comment when the silence becomes unbearable.

"Never mind the weather report," Mama snaps. "This is the third day in a row you don't even hear the alarm. It's over a month now that we've tried out your plan, and every morning, it's harder and harder for you to get out of bed."

She's just dying for me to concede that I've taken on more than I can handle. Fat chance, I say to myself. But I know I'll only make matters worse if I try to defend myself. So instead, I just gulp down my cereal in silence, and keep my fingers crossed that Aunt Yo will show up soon to relieve the tension. Following this wonderful start, things only get worse as the day progresses.

"You almost made Leona Carmichael a very happy woman," Mrs. Kvares says to me. It's midafternoon and she's reviewing my payroll figures.

"Huh?" I respond absently, barely looking up. For the first Friday since I started working for Miller and Son, I'm worried I won't be able to finish the payroll on time.

"Well, according to you, Mrs. Carmichael earned two thousand four hundred fifty-eight dollars and eighty cents last week." Mrs. Kvares' tone is only mildly caustic. Her expression, though, is the one she usually reserves it for those times when she contemplates the horrifying prospect that her son might still be potting geraniums when he's forty.

"I'm sorry. I guess I put the decimal in the wrong place," I mumble sheepishly.

"You know bosses tend to frown on little slips like that," she says. "At least the last mistake you made was in Mr. Miller's favor," she points out.

"That's supposed to make it better?!" I feel like retorting. Instead, I just promise to do better from now on. The truth is, lately I have been making more than my usual quota of blunders. In fairness to her, Mrs. Kvares has been a pretty good sport about it. And whenever Junior drops by to see how my "batting average" is holding up, she keeps my "strikeouts" a secret from him.

"Are you sure you don't want any of this rice pudding?" she asks when we take our afternoon break. I think she's trying to chalk up my mental deficiencies to a poor diet. It's the third time today she's tried to force food on me.

Friday is usually the Great Wave's busiest evening. Tonight is no exception. Steve is running around so much he doesn't notice I'm on the brink of burnout. Through some miracle, I am hanging in there okay. That is, until these two couples enter and noisily park themselves at one of my tables. The minute I see them, I get this gut feeling that disaster is just around the corner. The four of them have come in a lot lately. Luckily, our other regulars are nothing like them. For one thing, most customers generally shut up when the show begins. At least through the first few bars, just to give the performer the benefit of the doubt. Not these characters. They don't even lower their voices until they've been shushed a dozen times. Steve calls them the Gang of Four. He likes them even less than I do. Everyone can tell they're pretty rich from the clothes they wear, but no one could guess it from the size of their tips.

I grit my teeth and walk over to them, determined to be pleasant. "Hi, would you like to see menus?" I ask, smiling.

"That's usually the way it's done," the blonde with the platinum streaks answers in this real snotty voice.

"Don't let the Gang of Four get you down," Steve says when we meet at the pick-up counter. "I had their number the first time they darkened our door."

I sigh, martyrlike.

"The women are the kind who plunge into a deep panic whenever their manicurist leaves town," Steve continues, warming to his subject. Their order has arrived. Instead of rushing to them with it, I stick around for Steve to finish. "The guys would sell their grandmothers into slavery for a date with the Playboy Bunny of the Year."

I notice the heavier of the two guys signalling impatiently to Larry. Oh, oh, he's going to complain about my slow service, I worry. I pick up my tray and make a beeline for their table. I'm almost there when I'm forced to zigzag abruptly to avoid colliding with a customer on his way to the john. A swift second later, my premonition comes true. I lose my balance and topple my tray, spilling two espressos with lemon peel on the floor, one Tab on the Gang of Four's table, and a cappucino all over the blonde's silk jumpsuit. She howls like she's been maimed for life. I stand there paralyzed while her date barks at me. Finally Jessica comes to my rescue. As she leads me away, Larry practically does handstands in order to calm them down. But he doesn't make much progress, at least not in the amount of time it takes Jessica to usher me into her office.

Once her door is safely shut, I burst into tears. Between sobs, I manage to repeat the words "I'm sorry" over and over.

"Alicia, it's not a tragedy," Jessica says in that soothing voice of hers. She hands me a box of tissues. I blow my nose, grateful she's letting me off the hook so easily. Then something inside me snaps and I break into fresh sobs.

"Alicia, calm down," she says a little more firmly. "Just take a deep breath."

I do as she says. It doesn't completely do the trick, but the worst is over. "Lately, it seems that all I ever do is say I'm sorry,"

I explain once I've finally gotten a grip on myself.

"Been messing up?" she asks sympathetically.

"And how," I nod. I tell her about my increasing immunity to alarm clocks, and how even basic arithmetic has begun to stump me recently.

To my relief, she doesn't seem to think my condition is irreversible. "You've been carrying a double load and you need a little breather," is the simple way she sums it up. Then she suggests I take the rest of the night off and grab some shut-eye.

"Oh, I'll be all right," I claim. She repeats her suggestion. Only this time it sounds a lot more like an order. I thank her, but before I leave I work up the courage to ask her if the strain I've been under has affected my singing.

"Not that I've noticed," she replies. "That isn't to say the strain won't eventually affect your performances. So it's important to take some time to recoup. There's something else you ought to kick around, Alicia: Any way you cut it, your schedule is rough. Expecting to carry it all off to perfection is the one sure way to make it even rougher." I must look puzzled, because she adds, "Come on, kid, surely

I'm not the first person to tell you you tend to be hard on yourself." She pauses patiently while I mull that one over.

"Not in those words, exactly," I answer uncertainly after a few moments. But now that she's brought it up, I do recall a comment Mr. Aarons once made. In fact, it had startled me so much that I'd memorized it verbatim. I was "laboring under a basic misconception regarding the nature of reality," he had claimed. Namely, that the world would come to an end if I made a mistake. That was not the case, he assured me.

"I used to think I had to be Superwoman, too," Jessica confides as she wraps up our talk. "Then I saw what it was doing to my disposition. I decided to come to terms with the fact that I was only human. You're still young now, Alicia, but someday you'll thank me for that advice."

I know Jessica is trying to help. And she does have a valid point. Going around tied up in knots all the time is no picnic. Believe me, if I could relax, I would. I just don't have the knack. Besides, it's easy enough for Jessica to tell me to cool it. She has it made. But I wonder how laid back she was when she was a young black girl growing up in the deep South. Not very,

I'll bet. Otherwise, chances are she would have never made it out of Louisiana in the first place. These days, she can put down being a Superwoman all she likes. But if you ask me, it was once her ticket to Paris.

On the downtown bus I try to recall the last occasion I heard the Superwoman rap laid on somebody. It startles me when I remember. Aunt Yo had said it last week when she came down on Mama for always working straight through her break. "Not even two minutes you take to stop for a soda!" she'd scolded her one night. "Hey, Superwoman, the boss is rich enough! When are you going to get that through your head?"

Mama set her straight. "The more pieces *you* finish, the more money *you* make. When are you going to get that through *your* head?" she retorted. Can't argue with that. I should know. If a week has gone by when Aunt Yo has earned more than Mama, it sure hasn't been since I've been making up the payroll.

"Yolanda, if I could afford to take a break, don't worry, I would," Mama added for good measure. Weird as it seems, maybe Aunt Yo was onto something when she claimed my mom and I were more alike than either of us realized.

Chapter 12

I guess all that talk about the resilience of youth isn't total hogwash after all. Because by the time the weekend is over, I'm not feeling wiped out any longer. All it took was sleeping well past noon on Saturday and a little later on Sunday. Mama's a real stickler for regular mass attendance, so I was afraid she'd be irritated with me when I didn't join her on our weekly trek to the Church of the Holy Redeemer. Still, she made no effort to hustle me out of bed.

"Alicia, you got some real color back in your cheeks," Aunt Yo exclaims when she and Mama return from the last service. By this time, I've made it out of bed, but I'm still lounging around the kitchen in my nightgown.

To my surprise, Mama agrees with Yo. "See, I knew Saint Jude wouldn't let me down. I lit a candle to Saint Jude for you," she explains offhandedly. Saint Jude is the patron of "Impossible Cases." I notice that Mama prays to him a lot.

"Thanks, Ma. You're a peach," I kid her. She shrugs as if to say, "Don't mention it." I know it sounds corny, but I'm sort of touched that she sprung some of her hard earned money to light a candle for me. I'm so busy griping about the times she gets on my case that sometimes I forget all the ways in which she shows me how much she cares about me.

"They don't have a statue of Saint Genesius at Holy Redeemer, or I would have lit a candle to him for you," Aunt Yo assures me. Genesius is the saint in charge of show biz folk.

"Holy Redeemer knew what they were doing," Mama retorts before I can tell Aunt Yo that it's the thought that counts. "This neighborhood has a lot more hopeless cases then it's got up and coming stars," she elaborates. Her voice is deadpan, but her eyes are twinkling.

By evening, I'm feeling strong enough to tangle with a new song melody. I haven't made enough money to restring my guitar the way I'd like to. But at least I've been able to replace the really hopeless strings.

I have to admit that's been a big morale boost.

I have ideas for a couple of songs about the Lower East Side. I'd like to weave some of the themes from Papa's folk music into them. He knew dozens of Puerto Rican folk songs. When I was a baby, he'd entertain me by singing them for hours on end. Not that he had any choice. Whenever he tried to stop, I'd beg for just one more.

Sometimes Mama would join him. They'd do duets, harmony and all. She seemed as if she were having a ball. To see her today, you'd swear I was making it up. Now she never sings. She doesn't even hum. Once I asked her about Papa's songs. But she just got this real sad look in her eyes. Then she claimed she didn't remember them. So if I want to use the folk material, I'll have to remember it on my own, I guess.

I always have ideas for songs to spare. Composing them is another story. I don't exactly knock a song out. It's always a slow and painful process.

Steve keeps reassuring me that that'll change, if and when I get formal training. I haven't had any so far.

If I had to rate myself, I'd say lyrics are my strongest point. I know I have a long way to go. But here and there, I manage to come up with something halfway original.

My melodies are just okay. I wouldn't count on Marvin Hamlisch losing any sleep if he heard them. "Easy on the ears" is probably the best thing anyone can say about them. That's what Steve said about them, and he's a fan.

Working out chord arrangements is my biggest hassle. My technique is strictly trial and error, with the emphasis on error. I've spent many a winter night holed up in my room searching for a passable chord. When spring rolls around, I park myself on the stoop and plunk away there. But no matter how long I slave, no one could rave about the final result.

Sometimes I wonder how Mrs. Reuben puts up with me. Regardless of how many clinkers I hit, she remains at her window post. She has never once complained. For a while I figured she was hard of hearing. But that doesn't jibe with her semi-official status as block historian. It probably has to do with the fact that if Mrs. Reuben can put up with the same job for thirty-seven years, she can put up with anything.

This Sunday evening, I'm making pretty decent headway on my latest song. Aunt Yo has persuaded Mama to take a walk, so I have the apartment to myself. My new song is called *New England Camp*, and I have Robin to thank for the subject matter. Her latest disaster bulletins from New Hampshire have given me tons of material.

But the minute Mama and Aunt Yo return to the apartment, my concentration starts to waver. That's because one of their great debates is in full swing. Inez Marin and Yolanda Rivera have been known to squabble about practically anything. But certain subjects definitely get special play — the men Aunt Yo dates, for example. That's the topic currently raising their blood pressure.

When Yo and her husband Miguel first split, Yo's theme song was "Give me the single life any day." Lately though, she's made no bones about the fact that she's looking for a replacement. So far, only a couple of candidates have earned Mama's seal of approval. Tomás Machado, Aunt Yo's most recent boyfriend, hasn't even come close. I knew he didn't stand a prayer, not after he took her dancing on the Staten Island Ferry. It doesn't take much to make my mother write someone off.

"So what if he's crazy about you?" I hear Mama say over the water she is running to make coffee.

"What do you mean, 'so what'? You don't think that matters?"

I don't blame Aunt Yo for sounding incredulous. If a guy were nuts about me, I'd overlook a few minor flaws, too. Even hardhearted Robin admits that craziness counts.

"So he pays you a lot of compliments."

"You make it sound like a crime."

By this time, I've laid down my guitar.

"Just remember," Mama continues, quoting the Book of Esperanza, "the smoother the tongue, the smaller the bankbook."

That does it as far as Aunt Yo is concerned. She retorts with rapid-fire speed. Since she's switched to Spanish, I have a little trouble following her. But I manage to catch the gist of what she's saying. Namely that the Book of Esperanza has always been one big downer, cover to cover.

I can't make out my mother's reply. Not only is she talking fast and in Spanish, but her tone is muffled. Aunt Yo's comeback is also hushed. I decide to take another stab at *New England Camp*. But before I know it, I hear my mother's voice ring out in English loud and clear: "Just because she looks a little better today doesn't change my mind. I still think Alicia is trying to do too much."

I play louder in order to drown her out, but my heart isn't in it. I lay my guitar down again, just in time to hear Mom complain, "It's not enough, all those hours in the coffee house. The little she's home, she sits in her room and plays all the time."

"And for this you complain? Inez, your problem is you don't know when you're well off. You heard yourself what Aunt Fernanda said last week: 'For a daughter like Alicia, I would give all my gold fillings.' And she's got more than a few," Aunt Yo points out. "Or maybe you would like it better if Alicia took drugs like Carlos, or got herself a baby?"

Aunt Yolanda, bless your heart. When I make it, I'm going to mention you on every talk show they book me on. I'll tell people about all the times you stood up for me. You're going to get thanked coast to coast.

"I'll tell you what I like better, Yolanda," my mother snaps. "That Alicia comes down to earth. That she finds herself a good job."

I'm beginning to worry that my days at the Great Wave are numbered, that Mama is working herself up, and any moment now, she will march into my room and order me to quit the coffee house.

As it turns out, Aunt Yo has the identical fear. "Oh, come on, Inez, let Alicia stay at the coffee house a little longer," she coaxes. Silence follows. Mama really *is* considering handing me my pink slip. My heart starts thumping. My palms sweat. After what seems an eternity, she says, "Finish your coffee, Yolanda, before it gets cold."

My sigh of relief can be heard clear across the Williamsburg Bridge. That's as close as Mom will come to conceding she's let Aunt Yo win this round. For the moment, I'm safe. But I'm not taking any chances. Next week, I'll make sure to get to mass. I'll even go Mama one better and light *two* candles to Saint Jude. Just to be on the safe side. Jude may be an old hand when it comes to Impossible Cases and all, but asking him to change Inez Marin's mind is asking him to take on an overtime job. Knowing how stubborn my mother can be, I might even be handing Jude the challenge of his career.

Chapter 13

By the time next Sunday has rolled around, though, I'm afraid it'll take a lot more than a couple of candles to Saint Jude to turn the tide in my favor. The week began uneventfully enough. My roller coaster ride didn't really get underway until Wednesday. Once things started to happen, though, they just kept careening out of control.

On Wednesday morning, my day at Miller and Son begins as usual. I step out of the elevator and walk down the hallway, minding my own business. Suddenly, Mr. Miller pops up out of nowhere. After wishing me good morning, he says, "Now that we've cleared the mid-season mark, Alicia, it's time for us to have a confidential talk."

This throws me for a loop. For starters, Miller, Junior isn't exactly someone I feel comfortable shooting the breeze with. I feel myself tensing as he ushers me into the turquoise inner sanctum. Considering I'm such a slow starter in the mornings, I hope I manage to string together an intelligible sentence here and there. I needn't have worried, not about that anyhow. As it turns out, Junior does most of the talking. "Mr. Miller, Senior, always made it a company policy to hire minorities. He felt very strongly about the subject," Junior begins. He sounds very solemn. "When I took over, I assured Mr. Miller, Senior that I would continue that tradition. I think you'll agree I've kept my word," he says proudly.

And how! Whenever I flip through the names on the payroll, it reads like a regular United Nations roll call. Besides Puerto Ricans, Cubans, and Dominicans, there are Greeks, Philippinos, and Haitians. And that's just a random sampling. Still, Junior and Senior haven't exactly done something to put them in line for the Nobel Peace Prize. I mean it's not like they chose Aunt Yo, Mom, and the Pappaleo sisters over the swarms of Rockefellers who were breaking down their doors in search of a job.

"But in my book, it's not enough to hire minorities in entry level jobs. Whenever possible, I like to upgrade their status,"

he continues. "Believe it or not, you're looking at someone who hasn't lost faith in the
melting pot ideal. It's an employer's duty
to assist his ethnic wage earners' entry into
the American mainstream." He's beginning to sound more and more like he's running for office. He leans forward and
continues easily, "To give promising, but
disadvantaged youngsters like yourself the
break in life they deserve."

*Want to give me a break? Let me out of
here.* The worst thing about being "disadvantaged," as Junior puts it, is the number
of "advantaged" dodos you have to listen
to.

"You have a very quick mind, Alicia,"
Junior tells me. Not quick enough to find a
way to make you shut up, I think ruefully.

"Quick enough to have a career in accounting. I'm not flattering you," he adds.

You don't say. It's not like he's calling
me Avenue A's answer to Einstein. Then I
say to myself, Cool it, Marin. Where do you
come off having such a swelled head?
Lately, you're lucky to be quick enough
to catch your mistakes in time.

"But you'll never become a C.P.A. unless," Miller Junior pauses dramatically,
"unless," he repeats, "you set your mind
to it."

Well, I guess that settles that. No way, José.

"The choice is yours, Alicia."

I sure hope so.

"However, if you do decide to go for it, we might be able to work something out," he says with a mysterious smile.

I still don't know what he's getting at, but I'm thinking that maybe I have been a little hard on the guy. No doubt about it, Miller the Younger is corny. Still, you have to give him credit for being sincere. He probably makes large pledges to all the telethons on TV.

"Chances are, I can find you an opening on a farm team," he continues. "If you show promise, after one season, you'll have a crack at the Major Leagues." And here *I* was worried about being intelligible. Junior may be sincere, but *what is he talking about?* "Of course, I'm not going to lay my cards on the table until you decide how you're going to play your hand. So kick it around a bit, Alicia. The ball's in your corner now."

Kick what around? If the ball's in my corner, consider it dropped, I feel like cracking. I mean, deciding how to play your hand can be a little tough when you've been given zero idea of what cards you're holding.

Instead I say, "I will, Mr. Miller." He smiles one last time, then glances briskly at his watch. That's my cue that our confidential talk is over. I gratefully spring to my feet and make a bee-line for the door.

"Just remember, Alicia," Junior calls to me the moment my hand has grasped the doorknob. I let go and turn to face him. "People become successful in life not because they're smarter, uh-huh," he shakes his head, "but because they make choices — and stick to them." His delivery is calm, but you know he's dead serious.

"That's what our guidance counselor told us this semester," I answer solemnly as I leave his office.

At lunchtime, as I think about my confidential talk with Junior, I remember Mr. Aarons' words in the spring. Basically they boiled down to, you make your choice, give it your best shot, and if you hang in there long enough there's bound to be a payoff.

"Even if you made the wrong choice?" I had wondered out loud once the bell had rung and Steve, Robin, and I were walking to our next class.

"Especially, if you made the wrong

choice," Steve piped up. As usual, he was being a smart aleck.

"I think it's all a big waste of time," Robin declared flatly.

"What is?" I asked.

"Discussing things in the abstract." For once she sounded more exasperated than blasé.

"I don't want to get too abstract here, Robin," Steve said mildly, "but the ability to conceptualize is one of the major factors separating humans from the lower forms." His face had only traces of a smirk.

"I don't care. A theory has never helped anyone cope," Robin answered disdainfully. "Not when a person actually has a problem and has to make a decision."

"Then how does a person make a choice? Besides flipping a coin?" Steve asked.

"I don't know. It varies from case to case." She shrugged. "Fear, gut instinct, how much money they have in the bank. But what they believe in the *abstract* doesn't enter into it at all," she maintained. "*That* much I'm sure of."

Once she'd said her piece, Robin became her usual laid-back self again.

Tonight, while I'm sitting on my bed brooding, I admit I really have to hand it to Robin. She doesn't go out on a limb very often. But when she does, she usually has a point.

You may think you know how you'll react in a crisis. But when you come face to face with one, I'm afraid it's (as Mr. Miller, Junior, would put it) a whole different ballgame. I'm finding that out the hard way.

Chapter 14

By Wednesday night, the situation becomes even more complicated. A stranger throws me a curve ball that makes me forget all about my puzzling conversation with Junior, temporarily anyhow.

The Upper East Side is supposed to be deserted in August. Everybody who can afford to, takes off for the seashore or the mountains. But you'd never guess this from the size of the audience at the Great Wave this Wednesday night. The joint is really packed.

When it's my turn to perform, I start with *Tar Beach* and end with *Carlos' Song*. Considering that my performance is nothing to write home about, the audience is very kind. Before I return to my station, Jessica takes me aside. A guy's standing next to her. I'd say he's in his late twenties. His blue jeans are faded and his boots look custom-made. ("A combination that's a sure sign of affluence," Steve commented later.)

"Alicia, this is Warren Adler," Jessica says. "Warren's producing a musical at the West Side Arts Theatre."

"It's an update of 'Rio Rita,' with additional music," Adler explains after he's said hello, or hi, to be more precise. His smile is real mellow.

"Oh," I reply, trying to sound like I'm familiar with both the West Side Arts Theatre and "Rio Rita," neither of which is the case.

"I really enjoyed your act tonight. There's a part in the show you're very right for," he tells me.

Is this really happening? Since I've been at the Great Wave, I've received tons of compliments. But until tonight, that was all. My adrenaline starts working overtime. As it turns out, I was jumping the gun.

"We're holding auditions tomorrow from ten to five. I'd like you to call the stage manager and set up an appointment," Adler says. "That is, if you're interested." From his breezy manner, you can tell he doesn't have too many doubts on that score.

He's right. Okay, it may not be a firm

offer but it's still a chance to audition for a musical on the New York stage! To be blunt, my first chance. "Yeah, I'm interested." I didn't want to come off like an eager beaver, but I'm afraid I overdid it. I sounded a little too nonchalant. "I'd love to audition, Mr. Adler," I add. This time I sound a little too perky. Striking the right balance can pose a real problem for intense types like me.

He hands me his card. Underneath his name, it says, "Libra Rising Productions." "Wow!" I exclaim, before I can catch myself. "What a great omen. Libra is my rising sign."

Adler smiles at me indulgently. Jessica looks amused. I feel like a jerk. That's not a good omen.

"I can't believe I said that," I tell Steve as we ride home later.

"I can," he answers sarcastically. He thinks astrology is bunk. "But, Marin, I wouldn't worry too much about sounding silly. I mean any guy who'd name his company Libra Rising is begging for comments like that."

"Well, at least he didn't name his company Adler and Son or Libra Rising and Son of Libra Rising."

We've pretty much exhausted that subject, so we switch to more basic matters. "I can't believe I didn't ask Adler anything about the part," I wail.

"I can't believe it either. Just make sure you get all the details from the stage manager when you call him tomorrow morning," Steve cautions me.

"Uh-hùh," I promise. After a beat, I ask, "Steve, Adler said the show was an update of 'Rio Rita.' " Does that mean they plan to do it as a spoof?"

" 'Rio Rita' already is a spoof." Steve sighs wearily at what he considers one more example of my alarming ignorance. Not being up on every single 1940's camp musical does not mean a person's dimwitted, but you'd never guess that from the expression on Steve's face. You'd think I had asked him if Napoleon had been named after the French pastry or whether it was the other way around.

It goes without saying that Steve also has the scoop on the West Side Arts Theatre. It's an off-off Broadway theater with a growing reputation for mounting first-rate showcases. A few recent productions received reviews good enough to enable them to move to larger theaters. One show even moved to Broadway where it is still playing to full houses.

That's all I need to hear. Broadway! Of course the concert stage will always be my first love. But if Linda Ronstadt can spend a year doing *The Pirates of Penzance* on Broadway, then who am I to rule out a season on the Great White Way?

I start imagining the huge billboard advertisement for the show. It'll be plastered all over town. Needless to say, my image dominates it. My smile is dazzling, my lips cherry red, my wide brimmed hat decorated with cherries — also bananas, grapes and a couple of tangerines. By the time we reach 23rd Street, I'm working on my acceptance speech for the Tony Awards. Steve tries to bring me back to earth.

"Would you like me to go with you tomorrow?" he asks.

"If it won't hang you up or anything," I reply casually. I thought he'd never ask.

"I don't have anything special planned." He shrugs.

"I'll call you after ten," I tell him. "Soon as I reach the stage manager."

We'd already discussed my taking off from work. I told Steve I didn't think Mrs. Kvares would give me a hard time. In fact, if Junior raised his eyebrows, she'd probably make up an excuse to get him off my back.

We get off the bus and walk east. The air is very muggy. The usual crowd is hanging out in front of Raoul's candy store. And as usual, they're joking and carrying on like they're having the time of their life.

You couldn't call them bad kids. They don't have police records and they'd come through for you in a crisis. On the other hand, you couldn't exactly call them overachievers. Mama's already labeled them the drifters. I told her I thought that was a little harsh considering they're only seventeen.

"Never mind," Mama said. "I see it in their eyes. Ten years from now, they'll still be standing on the sidewalk outside of Raoul's," she predicted.

I wonder. Sometimes I envy them because they seem so carefree. But when you get right down to it, I wouldn't want to trade places with them. It scares me just to think that I might drift away my best years hanging out.

Luckily I don't think that's going to happen. "Everything's going pretty much according to plan," I say as Steve and I turn the corner onto my block. "And you set it all in motion, pal." I tend to take Steve for granted, so I figure expressing a little gratitude now and then won't kill me. "After all, you were the one who shamed me into auditioning for Jessica." I remind him of the "Nothing will get you nowhere faster than a no-show" number he rammed down my throat. "If it weren't for that, I might have chickened out," I admit.

It's funny. I was really tied up in knots at the time. It's hard to believe that was only two months ago. Performing at the Great Wave has given me a lot of confidence. I guess I'm bound to develop a minor case of the jitters once I arrive at the theater tomorrow, but I doubt I'll be incapacitated by my nerves.

Steve is strangely quiet. When we arrive at my building, we stop at my stoop for a moment. "Alicia, this Adler asking you to try out, it's a good break and all," he begins thoughtfully. "I don't blame you for being excited. . . . " His voice trails off.

"Who's excited? Don't worry," I assure him. "Like my grandmother said, 'Don't fry your bananas while they're still green.' "

"Auditioning for a specific part — well,

it's a different situation from the one at the Great Wave." Steve sounds so gentle it's almost as if he's walking on eggshells.

"Steve, please. What do you take me for? I *know* it's a long shot." I sound so convincing that I almost convince myself.

"Just checking," Steve replies. He seems relieved. "See you *mañana, señorita*." He smiles and is off.

I enter the building. Usually by the time I check in at night, I barely have the strength to plod up the stairs. Tonight, I have so much energy I could dash up all three flights. Nothing recharges my batteries better than the prospect of fame and fortune just around the corner.

Despite what I said to Steve, I happen to think my odds are a lot better than I let on. Sure, other girls will be auditioning for my part. But how many of them got to perform their act before the show's producer the night before? That alone should tip the scales in my favor. I mean the guy really dug me and I wasn't even in top form.

As I approach the apartment, I hear music coming from the door. What's going on? It's a quarter to twelve and Mama has Tito Puente on the phonograph?

People's voices can be heard as well.

Sounds of laughter, too. No doubt about it. A party's in session. It's not in character for Mama to kick up her heels this way, especially on a week night. Either she's flipped out or she's won the sweepstake. I fumble for my key, eager to find out which.

Chapter 15

By the time I open the door, I've discarded the sweepstake theory. Mainly because I've remembered Mama never buys lottery tickets.

I lean against the inside door and glance down the hall. Great Uncle Paco is the first person I see. He is mamboing to the Tito Puente cut. Paco's no Fred Astaire, still he's pretty nimble considering he's up there in years. Whatever he lacks in timing, he compensates for in enthusiasm.

Next I notice his dancing partner. Believe it or not, the woman executing the fancy sidestep with flawless grace is Inez Marin! She has natural flair, the kind you can't fake. What's more, she's singing along to the music, trills and all. Her voice has a pretty, lyrical quality. It's high pitched, but even and well sustained. The

biggest shock is how carefree she looks —
like a young girl, at least from where I'm
standing. She certainly is a far cry from
the Inez Marin I see every day.

They're having such a ball they don't
even hear me enter.

"Inez, how come you keep it a secret that
you got such a pretty voice?" Uncle Paco
teases.

"Maybe because it's the first time in
years that I got something to sing about,"
she answers liltingly.

Something is definitely up. The question
is *what?* I take a few tentative steps toward the living room. Mama and the others
turn and see me.

"Alicia, *querida*!" my great Aunt Fernanda gushes as she makes a beeline towards me and hugs me to her bosom. She's
got a bosom like a Wagnerian soprano.
She comes on as strong as one, too. "Congratulations!" she says fervently.

Now I'm really thrown for a loop. How
in the world did they hear about my "Rio
Rita" audition? Did Jessica call with the
news? Has Mama finally realized she's been
selling me short all these years? Did she
throw this party to make amends?

Aunt Fernanda is holding me so tightly
I'm having difficulty breathing. I finally

extricate myself. But before I can find out why she's congratulating me, Uncle Paco approaches me, arms extended. "Come on, *niña*. Give your old Uncle Paco a kiss," he says, beaming. I oblige. From the corner of my eye, I notice an uncut cake, and wine and soda laid out on the table. Mama has really gone all out. But why?

I also see Aunt Yo for the first time. She is perched against the windowsill. Compared to the others, she seems strangely subdued. What a switch!

Paco finally lets me go after giving me two big wet kisses — one for each cheek. "What's going on?" I ask.

"You make your mama so happy she give a party for you!" Fernanda exclaims. Some people end all their sentences with question marks. Everything Aunt Fernanda says has an exclamation point at the end of it.

"Mama. . . ." I look toward my mother helplessly. I'm growing more puzzled by the second.

Instead of answering right away, Mama just stands there. Then she drops her bombshell. "Mr. Miller wants to send you to college!"

"Huh?" *What is she talking about?*

"How do you like that!" Aunt Fernanda

interjects. I can see she's going to add her two cents every chance she gets. I just wish she'd shut up long enough for Mama to explain.

"Mr. Miller wants you to keep on working at the company part-time when school starts this September," Mama continues. Now that she's broken the ice, her words tumble forth. She's so excited you'd almost think she *had* won the lottery. "And Mr. Miller wants you to take an accounting course at night — at Baruch College."

Mr. Miller wants? It's the third time she's said that in as many seconds. *What about what I want, Mama?*

"They have a special program there for high school seniors who are good in math," she continues blithely. "And here's the best part, Alicia." I brace myself. "After you graduate, Mr. Miller will pay for you to go to evening college!" she says exuberantly.

"To major in accounting," Uncle Paco adds. He makes it sound like international banking.

"And during the day, you work for him permanently," Mama continues. She isn't merely smiling — she's positively radiant.

Miller, Junior's plans for me have left me speechless. I mean, when could any of this have happened? My second confidential talk with Junior took place only this morning. He had something up his sleeve, sure. But at no time did he utter a single statement that could possibly have been construed as a specific course of action. Besides, didn't he ask me to mull it over or to kick it around or however it was he put it? I do remember his saying the ball was in my corner. Was I wrong in thinking that meant I got to make the next move? Then how could he have gone and laid out this detailed plan to my mother?

"When did you talk with him?" I ask warily.

"This afternoon," my mother answers. "Just before the day was over. Mr. Miller came right on the factory floor and he asked me to come to his office with him." Her voice is so full of awe you think he'd parted the Red Sea. "At first I thought it was bad news." She smiles.

It was, Mama. In my book, anyhow.

"The first person in our family to go to college," Aunt Fernanda says proudly.

Wait a minute! Hasn't it dawned on anybody to ask me if I want to go along with this?

By now I'm so rattled I can't think straight. The Tito Puente record is still blaring on the phonograph. And the glare from the overhead lamp is so harsh it irritates my eyes. The room has taken on a nightmarish quality. And when I squint at Aunt Fernanda and Uncle Paco, their grins seem to have broadened into leers.

Uncle Paco lifts his wine glass and toasts me: "To my little niece, Alicia. She's not only pretty but smart." Then Aunt Fernanda shoves a plate with an enormous piece of cake on it at me. "Here, have a piece of cake. You gonna need your strength." She breaks into this raucous laugh. She sounds as mirthless as a carnival fat lady stationed at the entrance of the House of Horrors.

But the worst is yet to come. "Of course, the first thing Mr. Miller wants you to do is forget about your singing and the coffee house," Mama says.

It takes a couple of moments before her words register. That's partially because of the offhand manner in which she's sprung this on me. To hear her, you'd think it was some minor detail, hardly worth mentioning.

There is another reason I'm having difficulty believing my ears. Even Junior couldn't have that much gall. Deciding my future with a wave of his hand — and then informing my mother rather than me?! What's *really* weird is that I had no idea Junior even knew about my job at the Great Wave. He certainly never let on that he did. Yet just like that he thinks he can order me to quit.

I sink into the armchair. A hundred thoughts race through my mind. When I finally speak, my voice sounds dull. "Mr. Miller said he wanted me to quit the coffee house?"

"Of course he does." To Mama his demand is perfectly understandable. "He wants you there steady — not any minute you're gonna run off and be a singer," she says. She makes becoming a singer sound as savory as running off to join a band of international pickpockets.

Suddenly my head starts throbbing. I feel paralyzed.

"I don't want to do it, Mama," I say in a quiet but surprisingly firm voice.

She blinks. "What?"

"I said I don't want to do it," I repeat, a shade more emphatically.

Mama stares at me uncomprehendingly. "Alicia, you think a break like this comes along every day?" But instead of nailing me with her disapproving stare, she looks confused and panic-stricken, like a cornered fawn.

Aunt Fernanda has stopped chortling; her expression is now gloomy but fierce. Uncle Paco retreats sheepishly into a corner. When storm clouds appear on the horizon, he usually tries to get as far as possible from the eye of the hurricane. Yolanda calmly sips her wine, but I notice she's frowning.

It's only been a few short minutes since I walked in the door, but already the party has fizzled. I feel like a heel for ruining everybody's fun. But before I allow my feelings of guilt to overwhelm me, I remind myself that I have something at stake. My life, namely.

I bolt out of the chair. "Tonight a producer was in the audience at the Great Wave, and after he heard me sing, he asked me to audition for the musical he's producing — "Rio Rita.""

"No kidding, *querida*," Yo says enthusiastically.

Aunt Fernanda and Mama shoot synchronized angry glances at her. Stop encouraging her, their expressions say.

"It's going to be at the West Side Arts Theatre, off-off Broadway," I continue.

From the proud note in my voice, you'd think I had said the Kennedy Center. But then, this is no time to be modest.

"Because you have an audition, you want to turn down a permanent job and a chance to go to college?" Mama asks incredulously. Her initial panic has blossomed into full-scale alarm.

"Mama, I'm going to be a singer," I say in even and rational tones. "So I don't need Mr. Miller to send me to college."

"You're crazy," she snaps. "She's crazy," she repeats for the guests' benefit.

Aunt Fernanda bobs her head up and down in instant agreement.

"I am not."

"Oh, no? You think that because you sing in a coffee house you're going to become a star?" Mama scoffs.

Once again, Fernanda provides a quick back-up. "You got your head in the clouds, young lady," she thunders. She turns to Uncle Paco and mutters, "Alicia is just like her father." Aunt Fernanda is far from my favorite relative and comments like that are part of the reason.

Aunt Yo also considers Fernanda a royal pain. She tries to come to my rescue. "Why shouldn't Alicia become a singer if that's what she wants to do? Or maybe you think only rich people have a right to make music?" she counters.

"You mind your own business," Fernanda bellows. "You never had no common sense neither."

Uncle Paco, the peacemaker, timidly steps out of the corner. "Now, *niña,*" he says tenderly as he caresses my forehead.

I pull away from Paco. "Just leave me alone, everybody!" I turn toward my mother. "Look, I'm not interested in Mr. Miller's offer. Not if I have to give up my music, Mama."

My mother doesn't reply. She just looks at me vacantly as if I've taken leave of my senses. This ticks me off so much my voice turns shrill. "Can't you understand?"

Obviously not, because she just shakes her head and says bitterly, "You're gonna mess up your life." It's not the words I mind as much as her matter-of-fact delivery.

"Just because you don't think I'm talented doesn't mean everyone else agrees with you," I sputter.

But there is no getting through to the woman. Instead of answering me directly, she murmurs forlornly, "A once-in-a-lifetime offer. Anyone else would be grateful."

Grateful?! She's really going too far.

Okay, so it was decent of Junior to offer to spring for night school tuition. But I'm only sixteen. It's *not* my last chance, despite what Mama may think.

By this time I feel so hassled, I start questioning Mama's motives for throwing this bash in the first place. I doubt Aunt Fernanda was summoned to the apartment simply for the purpose of making whoopee. More likely, Mama felt her chances of bull-dozing me into accepting Junior's plan were vastly improved with Fernanda on the premises.

When Steve said, "Some were born to party, and some were born to brood," he'd overlooked a third category: Namely, those who thrive on throwing their weight around.

"You pass up the boss's offer," Aunt Fer-nanda warns me now, "I guarantee you, you gonna be sorry." She wags her finger in my face.

"I'll take that risk," I tell her.

"It's easy to say that when you're young," Mama begins.

But I've had enough. "Look, stop trying to railroad me. Just because you're grow-ing old working for Miller and Son doesn't mean I have to follow in your footsteps. My life doesn't have to be a dead end, too."

The instant the words are out of my mouth I regret them. Especially when I notice Mama wince. Our eyes meet for a split second, then she turns away. Aunt Yo is already facing the window. Paco lowers his eyes. There is silence.

It almost comes as a relief when Fernanda shouts, "You should be ashamed talking that way." It sure beats watching Mama's mouth twitch in tiny involuntary spasms. That's her way of fighting off tears. I know because I saw her do it a lot when Papa died.

Before Fernanda can deliver a full tongue lashing, I rush off to my room, mainly to avoid bursting into tears myself. As I close my door I hear Mama murmer, "I was so happy, I made a party . . ." Her voice trails off wistfully.

This time Fernanda happened to be right. I was way out of line. Mama had no business ramming Junior's plan down my throat, but where do I come off telling her that her life has been a dead end? Next to "It might have been," I think the second saddest words in any language are "Why did I say *that*?"

Of course, I don't doze off when I get into bed. I toss and turn. I shut the window to blot out street noises. Five minutes later,

I open it to get some air. Finally, instead of counting sheep, I chant "Keep your big mouth shut," over and over. I know it's pointless. But maybe it'll sink in for future reference. Right now, though, it does little to shut out the image that's keeping me awake: the pain I saw in Mama's eyes when I vowed I wouldn't end up like her.

Chapter 16

This is one morning no one would mistake Inez Marin for a talk show hostess. When I enter the kitchen, she sets a plate of scrambled eggs before me without so much as grunting hello. Her eyes have circles under them, guess she hasn't had a good night's sleep either.

I nibble halfheartedly at my eggs. Any moment now I expect my mother to order me into more appropriate white collar worker clothing. Taken on their own, there is nothing exotic about the blouse and skirt I am wearing. Once you add a print cummerbund, apple green stockings, hoop earrings, and a couple of fancy hair combs, though, my image is definitely more Brazilian bombshell than Baruch College bookkeeping student. But what can I do? Warren Adler said to call the "Rio Rita" stage manager this morning. I have no idea what time my audition will be, or whether there will be time to change beforehand. But Mama seems too distracted even to notice how I'm dressed. In fact, it's almost as if I'm not there. She concentrates on eating her eggs, taking hearty bites in contrast to my small ones.

I may be decked out pretty festive, but inside I still feel rotten about last night. I realize it's up to me to make the first move. Only I don't know how to go about patching things up. I guess saying I'm sorry is about as good a place as any to begin.

"Mama, last night, when I said —"

"Eat your eggs," she interrupts coldly.

I try, but I've completely lost my appetite. My ear remains glued to the outside door. When I finally hear Aunt Yolanda's stiletto heels clicking up the staircase, I breathe a huge sigh of relief. That staccato rhythm has never sounded more musical.

"So where are the castanets?" Mrs. Kvares comments after she gives me a quick once-over. I've just entered the office. I rapidly explain about the audition. Not only does she take it in stride; she actually seems relieved.

"For a second you had me worried," she cracks. "I was afraid you'd chucked it in at the Great Wave and were going to start moonlighting as a flamenco dancer."

Whatever time the stage manager wants me is fine with her, she says. Should Junior come snooping around, she assures me she'll come up with a plausible excuse. She does extract one condition. If I make it on the Great White Way, would I be kind enough to put in a good word for David with the Stage Hand's Union? "It's not artsy like Japanese flower arrangements, maybe, but the pay scale's triple."

Naturally I humor her. Once I hit the big time, I promise to move mountains on the kid's behalf. Actually, there is no way I would conspire with her to steer David into a job not of his own choosing. It's funny. She's so understanding when it comes to my career ambitions. But with her own flesh and blood, she's a hardliner. Typical.

I connect with the stage manager without a hitch. We settle on a three forty-five audition time. But I hit a snag when I try to draw him out about the character I'm auditioning for. He talks in shorthand — ingenue — soprano — late teens to early twenties — general's daughter — wholesome" is the most I can get out of him.

"You mean I'm not auditioning for the title role?" I ask.

I hear a snicker on his end. "Rio Rita is the name of a river," he says condescendingly. "As in Rio Grande, or Nile." Then he clicks off.

"I thought Rio Rita meant Rita from Rio de Janeiro," I wail to Steve as I call to inform him about the audition time.

"The show takes place in Texas, Marin," he explains.

"Now's a fine time to tell me."

"Why? What difference does it make?"

Before I can answer, he's figured it out. "So you got yourself rigged up like a Latin spitfire at Carnival time, huh, kid?"

"Don't be ridiculous," I say a little too emphatically. In response, he chuckles knowingly. We agree to meet in front of the theatre at three thirty-five.

All morning I keep my fingers crossed that Junior won't drop by the bookkeeping office. I have enough on my mind without having to face him. At noon I sprint to the ladies room and take off the hoop earrings, the hair-combs, and the cummerbund. After careful deliberation, I decide the green

stockings can stay. After all, not every ingenue has to be a Marie Osmond clone.

I cut short my lunch break in order to
complete a batch of ledger entries by three.
Scrambling to beat the clock has its good
aspects. When you focus on petty details,
it keeps your mind off the larger issues.
When three rolls around, Mrs. Kvares orders me out of the office with instructions
to knock 'em dead.

As I wait by the elevators, I realize I'm
not nervous. That's good, I guess. But I'm
not excited either. That's weird. The problem is I still feel crummy about the night
before. Esperanza's warning to would-be
travelers pops into my head. "If you sail
away with bad blood on the shore, you're
asking for stormy weather."

Before I leave for the West Side Arts
Theatre, I try to patch things up with
Mama. She may not accept my apology.
But this time I won't let her stop me until
the words "I'm sorry" are out of my mouth.

To the left of the elevator bank is a
door to the stairway. The sign on it reads
"Factory — Two Flights Up." Before I
lose my nerve, I open the door and start
climbing. What with their peeling paint,
dusty air shafts and poor lighting, these
staircases to the factory area seem to me

a firetrap. Is this what Mama and Aunt Yo have to trudge up every morning?

I exit into the hallway. It's very different from Miller, Junior's executive suite. The din of the machines is deafening, the light is glaring, and it's hotter than the subway at rush hour in July.

"Gosh, what a rotten day for the air conditioning to break down," I remark to a young guy who stands outside a little cubicle of an office.

"That's real cute, kid," he says. "Hey, where you going?" he shouts gruffly as I continue on my way. It occurs to me that he might be a foreman. So I stop and say politely, "I'd like to speak to Mrs. Marin for a moment, please."

"There's no Mrs. Marin here," he barks. Civility isn't exactly his strong point.

"Yes there is," I respond evenly. "She's worked here for ten years." Who knows? Maybe he's new on the job. I might as well give him the benefit of the doubt. From the payroll, I know there are a lot of names to memorize, and very few of them easy to remember like Taylor or Smith.

"I'm one of the foremen, honey. I ought to know who works here."

So much for the benefit of the doubt. "Inez Marin," I explain. I'm starting to sound keyed up. Unless he stops giving me a hard time, I'm going to be late for the audition.

"Oh, Inez, one of the girls," he drawls. "Why didn't you say so in the first place?" Girls? *Girls?* I feel my stomach muscles tightening. Calling me honey was bad enough, but I don't have to deal with this bimbo on a day to day basis. My mother, the girl, does however.

Instead of being angry at him, I feel empty and embarrassed. My reaction confuses me. I mean he's the jerk, right? So how come *I* feel humiliated, as if I'd shrunk a couple of sizes right before his eyes? I don't get it.

There's another older guy sitting in the cubicle. "What do you want with her?" he asks as he beckons me to come closer. At least he sounds semi-human. I take a few cautious steps toward him. "I have to talk with her. It won't take long."

"Sorry, nobody's allowed on the floor during working hours," the young jerk says. But I don't answer. From the glass panel in the cubicle, I've caught my first glimpse of the factory area. I stare at the endless rows of sewing machines crowded one upon the other. The aisles are very narrow and in the whole vast space, there isn't a single window. A couple of overhead fans re-circulate the stale air.

The seamstresses are all bent over their machines, fingers flying as they rush to complete their daily quota. It's a regular United Nations in full session: West Indians, Asians, and Arabic women all working at breakneck speed. I find myself trying to match faces with the anonymous payroll names: Carmichael, Calabia, Feliciano, Kwa, Said. . . . Some are only teenagers while others are pushing sixty, but all of the women have the same concentrated, anxious look on their faces.

I freeze when I finally locate Mama. At home, she usually gives you the impression she has everything under control. Here she looks so vulnerable and defenseless, it's hard to believe it's the same person.

She's just pulled out a skirt from her machine and placed it on her completed pile. Now she pauses to brush a strand of hair off her forehead, then quickly fishes out an unsewn skirt piece from her basket, inserts it in her machine and begins stitching. Her fingers move confidently but her face has the same frightened look she had last night when I turned down Junior's offer.

"Is it important, kid?" I hear the older man say.

I turn to him, but I can't answer. I understand now that I'd only be making things worse by approaching Mama on the floor. I've realized why she placed the factory off limits to me. She was trying to protect me. It's hard to explain, but there's something scary about the place. It's not the noise, or the heat, or the crowded conditions, or even the hectic work pace. What's frightening is the sea of anxious faces, the rows and rows of "girls" all struggling to make their quota. It's as if a few dollars more or less in their paycheck is a matter of life and death to them.

Last night, Mama had flinched when I shouted that I wasn't going to end up like her. I wasn't going to grow old slaving away for *Miller and Son*. I didn't realize then how humiliating she found her job. It suddenly makes sense to me why being a bookkeeper seems like a really good deal to her.

I guess I must look pretty upset, because the older guy says, "Let the kid go in, Syd." "Inez is a good girl," he explains. "Not a troublemaker like some of the others." His words snap me out of my trance. What am I doing here? I've got to get out of this place. I've got to get to the theater. I back out of the cubicle. The foremen are looking at me like I'm weird. It doesn't matter. I just hope they don't say anything to Mama about my being up here.

"It's okay, forget it," I mumble. Then I turn and rush toward the staircase. None of this sweatshop stuff for me. I've got a crack at a role in a musical — and not just any role — the ingenue lead! Only I musn't blow it. I mustn't be late. I run down the rickety stairs so fast I almost trip three times before I finally hit the street.

Chapter 17

"Okay, that'll be all," the musical director says briskly. *All?* I've barely sung two bars of *Carlos' Song* and already he's giving me my walking papers? For this I waited an hour and a half in a sweltering lobby overflowing with other terrified females?! What a jerk I was to break my neck to get here on time!

Looking around at the competition, it was hard to figure out why the producer Warren Adler thought I was so right for the role. The other auditionees ranged in age from mid-teens to late twenties. Physically, the variety was even greater. They included petite snub-nosed blondes, tall freckled redheads and at least three Liza Minnelli look-alikes. When you got right down to it, the only thing we had in common was that we were female and under thirty.

I glance at the guys clustered around the musical director. Warren Adler is not among them. He would have set the guy straight — at least I think he would have — unfortunately he's nowhere in sight. "Peter, give her the 'Bandit Sweetheart' number," the M.D. now says to his assistant stage manager. I perk up. It looks like I'm still in the running. I'm not frying any bananas though. These guys are a cold crew, no two ways about it.

Peter thrusts a sheet of music into my sweaty hand. "Here, learn this," he orders me. The musical director was curt, but Peter is downright rude. Before I can reply, he ushers me into the back stage area.

"Norma, you're next," he motions to a tall dramatic looking brunette who's been standing in the wing area. Peter's snippiness doesn't faze her one bit. She follows him back on stage with a confident stride.

Now that I'm alone backstage, I notice the exit door. If I had any sense, I'd slip out through it. Marin, you nitwit, why didn't you tell them you can't read music, I wail to myself as I stare helplessly at my copy of "My Bandit Sweetheart." One, because Peter didn't give me the chance. Two, because I was afraid they'd slap handcuffs on me and charge me with fraud. Three, because I'm hoping against hope for a miracle to occur.

"My Bandit Sweetheart" looks like a fancy lyric soprano ballad. Unfortunately, that's all I can tell about it. Luckily I can overhear Norma as she launches into her rendition of the song. I have a pretty good ear so I softly hum along with her. I'm hoping that way I'll manage to nail down the melody. But before I can get the hang of it, they've cut her off. I don't know about these guys. She sounded pretty good to me.

A few seconds later, Peter is back. "They're ready for you now." Apparently, it didn't occur to any of them to ask whether I was ready for them. By the time I'm back onstage again, I'm kind of glad Adler isn't around to witness this fiasco.

The accompanist asks me what key I would like the song played in. This throws me for a loop. I can't very well say, "Same as Norma's," so in spite of my sneaking suspicion that it's way too high, I murmur, "The one it's in, please." This suspicion is confirmed when the pianist raises his eyebrows as if to say, "It's your funeral, kid."

As he plays the introduction, I fight off my growing sense of doom. I remember the pep talk Steve had given me earlier. "Whatever you do, Marin, don't be timid," he'd advised me. "If you're going to make a fool of yourself, do it on a grand scale. At least they'll remember you." Steve's suggestions usually have a lot of merit. Not this time, however.

A screechy off-key sound reverberates through the theater. It's close to the sound of chalk grating against a blackboard. To my horror I realize it's coming out of my mouth. Just as Steve had recommended, I've plunged into "My Bandit Sweetheart" in full voice. Or in loud voice to be more accurate. Full is about the last thing you could call my squeaky high notes.

The musical director and his cronies take about as long as they can, three bars to be exact. "We need a trained soprano for this role, Miss Marin," he says. His tone is polite but his smile is forced. I want to show him what a good sport I am. "I understand," I mumble magnanimously. For a second he peers at me intently. His smile turns into a smirk and I'm afraid he's about to say something very sarcastic. Instead, he just dismisses me with a nod.

I hurry toward the exit. By this time my cheeks are burning from shame. From the corner of my eye, I can see the musical director's face, his expression now long-suffering. "One of Warren's suggestions," an assistant says to him in a low but none-theless clearly audible voice.

"I wish he'd stick to fund raising," he replies.

I'd gladly give five years of my life not to have to walk through that lobby. Every-one in it will know I was the person re-sponsible for those screaming sounds they just heard. I lower my head and edge my way toward the front door without ever raising my eyes.

Steve is waiting on the theater steps. Good old Steve. I knew he'd still be there. Only I was wishing he wouldn't be. I didn't want to deal with him right now. Not him or anyone else.

"How'd it go?" he asks. You'd think he'd take a hint from the expression on my face.

"I don't want to talk about it," I snarl, and scoot on ahead of him.

He catches up to me at the corner. "Hey, Marin, where's the fire?"

"I just want to put as much distance as possible between me and that joint."

"That bad, huh?"

"I took your advice by the way," I inform him. "I made a big fool of myself — a very big fool."

The light changes. That doesn't prevent me from charging across the street. Steve bobs after me as I skirt the oncoming traffic. "It's not worth getting killed over," he says once we hit the sidewalk. I ignore him and continue walking.

Little by little, he cajoles me into filling him in on what happened. He isn't satisfied until I've told him each and every humiliating detail. And even then he doesn't have the decency to be horrified by my ordeal. In fact, he's so unruffled it's infuriating. I don't know why I'm surprised. Steve always manages to be cool — when it's someone else's trauma.

"Marin, even if you could read music, the part doesn't sound up your alley. So why not just chalk it up?" he says.

That does it. Next to the day Papa died, this has probably been the worst day of my life. And Steve has the nerve to tell me to chalk it up. I make an abrupt about-face and start walking in the opposite direction.

"Where are you going, Marin?" he yells.

"Home," I shout over my shoulder.

"But what about the Great Wave?" he asks as he catches up to me.

"Tell Jessica I have smallpox."

"Please! It was only one audition. You can't let it get to you this way," he cautions me. At least he's starting to look a little alarmed.

I stop walking and lean against a parked car. "I've been kidding myself, Steve."

"About what?"

"About thinking I could make it as a singer. You should have heard my competition. There were dozens of girls there — and they all had beautiful and trained voices. They could read music on the spot; they could belt *and* sing soprano; they had stage experience. A few had even been in Broadway plays."

"Okay, you weren't in their league," Steve concedes.

"In their league?! Don't be dense. I didn't even belong in the same room with most of them," I can see that I'm not getting through to him.

"So you learned something, today," he shrugs philosophically.

"You bet I did. I learned I don't stand a chance."

"Cool it, Marin. You learned that you need formal training. Something I've been telling you for ages." He just can't help rubbing that in. Typical.

"Okay. I guess I'll catch the next flight to Europe and hunt down the right vocal coach."

Steve makes an impatient gesture. "Give me a break. One little setback and you're ready to call it quits."

"I'd like to see how brave you'd be — without your father's money to fall back on," I retort.

Steve is silent for a moment. I can tell I've really hurt him. I look down at my shoes, embarrassed. So much for chanting, *Keep your big mouth shut* the night before.

"I know my family is better off than yours," Steve says finally.

"Look, I'm sorry," I tell him. "But I really need the night off. I'm too upset to waitress. I mean what if the Gang of Four shows up tonight and sits at my station? One false move on their part, and I might inflict permanent damage."

"So you're going to go home and brood, Marin?" Steve shakes his head wearily. "You have your heart set on it. I can tell."

"I'm just too beat, Steve. Jessica will understand."

He realizes my mind is made up. In a halfhearted way, he tells me to buck up. Then we go our separate ways.

Mama is surprised to see me. But she doesn't ask any questions. Not about the audition, not about why I'm not waitressing tonight. Her face is expressionless, except for her eyes. She makes no effort to mask their sadness. I lie and say I've already grabbed a bite with Steve. Then I head straight for my room.

I sit on my bed and stare out the window. My thoughts are so jumbled I'm having a hard time untangling them. Too much has happened today for me to absorb it all. It had been really weird going from Miller's factory floor straight to the West Side Arts Theatre. On the surface, the dressmakers and the singers are very different. Yet now that I'm finally alone and their images flash before me, I start to see a link.

First I see a long row of tired factory workers bent over their machines. Next, a row of anxious young singers lined up against the wall of the theater lobby. Suddenly their images become intermingled. The factory worker frantically stitching a skirt has Norma's face. The singer nervously mouthing the words to her song as she waits to audition turns out to be my mother.

Gradually the connection becomes clear. It's fear that binds them together. The dressmakers are afraid they won't make their quota. The singers are afraid they won't get the role. They both want things very badly; things they probably will never get. That's why fear has become such a constant in their lives. They try to hide it, but in one way or other, it's written all over their faces.

The singers at the "Rio Rita" audition, with their beautiful voices and good looks and fancy stage credits, were all still eager for a crack at a supporting role in an off-off Broadway musical. Every one of them wanted that part as badly as I did. But only one would get it. The rest would go on to the next audition, where they would again wait patiently for hours for the chance to sing eight bars of a song.

Even if I were in their league, is this the kind of life I want for myself? Mama had warned me last night, "Just because you sing in a coffee house, you think you're going to become a star. You're crazy, Alicia." I hate to admit it, but she was right. With no training, no money, and a second-rate guitar, I really have been living in a dream world.

Sure, maybe I could grab a weekend gig here and there, in some tacky nightclub. Basic expenses plus tips with a round trip bus ticket as the single costliest item on the expense tab. And if the audience really dug me, the owner would kick in an extra ten.

All in all, it would come to enough to keep me in breakfast cereal, but not much more. I'd have to scrounge around for a job as a waitress at the Market Diner to pay the rent on my furnished room.

I suppose I could mull the whole thing over for a few more hours. But what's the point, really? For once in my life, I might as well get something over with sooner rather than later. Maybe then I'll be able to get a good night's sleep.

I rise from the bed and walk to the kitchen. Mama's just finished washing the floor. She knows I'm there. Yet she slowly wrings out the mop before she looks up at me. "What is it, Alicia?" she asks.

"I've decided to take Mr. Miller's offer," I say without hesitation.

At first, she blinks disbelievingly, but when she realizes I'm serious, her face softens, and she silently acknowledges my words with a grateful smile.

Chapter 18

The next day I march right up to Junior's secretary. "I'd like to tell Mr. Miller in person that I've decided to accept his offer," I say to her. This is pretty classy of me, considering Junior's offer was not made person to person — his person to my person, that is.

My timing turns out to be terrific. A fabric shipment hasn't arrived, and Junior is busy raking the guilty party over the coals. So I'm spared the possibility of another confidential talk. Miller, Junior does interrupt his harangue long enough to "welcome me aboard." Things will turn out well, he assures me, as long as I'm with them "in spirit as well as in body." Don't ask for the impossible, kiddo, I think as he ushers me to the door and then quickly resumes reading the riot act to his underling.

* * *

"Are you crazy?" Steve says. He looks totally aghast. It's evening and I'm setting up my station at the Great Wave. He's come by to see how I am, and I've just sprung it on him that I've accepted my employer's offer.

"Yesterday, you were going to be a composer. Today, you're going to be a C.P.A.?" he asks incredulously.

I knew I should have waited until later to tell him. Now he's going to bug me all night. "I don't want to talk about it," I tell him. "Then why did you bring it up?" he answers logically. "I don't get it, Marin. You're shifting your whole life plan just because you bombed out at one lousy audition?" He seems genuinely bewildered.

"Not because I didn't get the part," I protest.

"Then why?" he persists.

"Because the audition gave me a clear view of what I'd be up against. You know as well as I do that I can't compete."

"Maybe today you can't," he acknowledges.

"Maybe not tomorrow or next year either," I say.

Steve shakes his head in disgust. "You know, Mozart didn't have it easy either.

But you didn't catch him crying uncle every time he hit a roadblock."

"Steve, you're really balmy. Mozart?!"

"Okay, Mozart was special. Maybe that's not such a good example," he concedes.

"Maybe not," I snicker.

"Okay, Marin," Steve says. "You aren't Mozart and you aren't a millionaire. Still, those are not good enough reasons to chuck it in."

"I decided to cut my losses. That's a plenty good reason," I maintain.

"At sixteen? What losses?" He is honestly perplexed.

"Excuse me. My sugar bowls need refilling," I say, and brush past him on my way to the kitchen. If I don't end this right now, he's liable to go on all night. He realizes I intend to stonewall him and he packs it in for the moment.

For the first time since I started working at the Great Wave, my heart isn't in my singing when I'm called on stage. The performance I give could be rated somewhere between routine and lackluster. Come to think of it, I wouldn't dish out rave notices to any of the Great Wave performers, not judging by tonight, anyhow. It's funny. Not long ago, I considered us all a very talented crew. Now I'm having second thoughts. I mean, our patrons get a floor show for the price of a cappuccino. Under the circumstances, it's only minimum courtesy to give the performers a nice round of applause. But how big an audience would we be drawing if they had to pay forty bucks to catch the act? Somehow I doubt we'd be packing them in at the rafters. I'm not putting us down. I'm just seeing the setup more clearly for the first time. To quote Aunt Yo on the subject of Tomás and his increasingly noticeable shortcomings: "The bloom is off my rose colored glasses."

During the bus ride home, for once in our lives, Steve and I have very little to say to one another. I mostly stare out the window. He finally takes out a book and opens it. For some reason, it's at this point that I suddenly feel compelled to make small talk. I guess the rift between us *is* making me uncomfortable. "What are you reading?" I ask.

"*Slaughterhouse Five,*" he answers. I guess I looked puzzled. "It's a novel by Kurt Vonnegut," he explains. "Ellie gave it to me. She said it was about time I read something else besides *Variety* and *Downbeat*." His tone is polite, but formal.

"Is it any good?"

"It's terrific," he says emphatically.

"Well, maybe I'll pick it up at the library one of these days," I comment absently.

"You really should, Marin," he begins coldly. "See, it's about this guy who made all the right choices. He did all the safe, conventional things expected of him. And guess what?" Steve gloats. "One morning he wakes up and discovers his life is a living hell!"

On that cheery note, Steve edges away from me a bit and buries himself in the next chapter.

Most of Saturday morning, I mope around my room. Somehow, the idea of working at the Great Wave tonight is making me edgy. I mean now that I've taken Junior up on his plan, it does seem kind of pointless to continue at the coffee house. In a few weeks, school will start. I'll have to quit then. So why not make a clean break now?

I decide to go up there and have a talk with Jessica. It would be a lot simpler if I quit by phone, but Jessica's been so nice to me I figure the least I can do is to tell her in person. I catch my reflection in my bureau mirror. Marin, what's this rush to burn all your bridges, I ask myself. Exactly why are you racing up to the Great Wave to call it quits a full two weeks before you have to? I don't have to search long for an answer. Working there is *painful*, not pointless. And the longer I stay on, the harder it'll be to cut the ties.

My guitar is propped against my desk. Just the sight of it bothers me. I pick it up and head for the closet. Suddenly I wonder what Papa would say if he could see me. In a funny way, I feel I'm betraying him. I clear out a spot for my guitar in the back of my closet and carefully place it down there. For good measure, I pile clothes on top of it. I want to be sure I won't come face to face with it every time I reach in for a pair of jeans. I shut the closet door. Then right on cue, I hear Mama knock. She comes in and looks at me hesitantly. Sometimes I forget just how shy she is. When she finally speaks, her voice is gentle.

"I know how you feel, *niña*," she says.

No, you don't, Mama. Because right now, I don't feel a thing. Sure I get these twinges. But I deal with them as they crop up. Want to know how I've felt these past few days? Numb, mostly. Like I've been injected with a huge novocaine shot. Hopefully, it'll last me for the next twenty years. By then, balancing the books is the only thing I'll ever get excited about.

"We all have to give up our drea_
sometime," Mama continues. "It hu_
at first, sure. But you made the righ_
choice."

How can I explain to her that I didn't
go along because I felt it was the right
choice. It was more like the only choice. Or
closer still, like I had no other choice.

"You'll see, *niña*. Soon you're going to
feel at peace with yourself," she says re-
assuringly. "I hope so, Mama." *But don't
hold your breath.* Deadened nerve ends is
one thing. Serenity is another.

When I get to the Great Wave, Jessica
doesn't exactly make quitting easy for me.
For starters, she's caught completely off
guard by my decision. She had the impression that I planned to make music my
career. So how come I changed my mind,
she asks. Lack of training, I answer. Only
she isn't buying.

"Alicia, training can always be ac-
quired," she says firmly. "You have the
main thing — talent. You know I'm level-
ing with you. I think you're an original."

Life sure has its quota of sneaky twists
and turns. Look at all the times I got upset
because my mother didn't think I could cut

Now I'm feeling lousy because Jessica believes I can.

"You don't understand, Jessica," I sigh. "My mother can't afford to send me to music school."

"You're right, Alicia. I don't understand," she replies. "If you wanted to go badly enough, you'd figure out a way to pay for your own training."

"It's not just the money, Jessica. My mother's dead set against my becoming a singer. Whenever I'd kid around about becoming a star, she'd tell me I wasn't playing with a full deck. The worst part," I add ruefully, "is that I've decided she's right."

Jessica smiles and takes a leisurely sip of her tonic water and lime. Then she adjusts a fold in the billowy white dress she's wearing. It always amazes me how cool she manages to look even in the middle of a heat wave. "So either you become a superstar — or you become an accountant? Is that how you see it, Alicia?" she asks.

"Well, not exactly," I admit.

"I didn't think so. You write songs because you need to express yourself. The applause is nice, sure. But it's secondary. That's one of the reasons your material isn't run-of-the-mill," she tells me.

This is so strange. I came here with mind made up. I have to make sure I do backtrack. "Jessica, I wasn't worried abou the applause. I was scared I wouldn't earn enough money to pay the rent."

"Naturally, there are no guarantees," she tells me. "But with the right training — with a music degree — you ought to be able to swing it."

I sigh. Despite my best intentions, I'm letting her sway me. "But where could I get training?" I ask.

"The City colleges are one possibility. They all have music programs and tuition isn't high," she tells me. "And when you start investigating one possibility, others usually pop up."

"You make it sound so easy," I whine.

"Easy, no. Possible, yes." she replies.

I feel as if some of my deadened nerve ends are becoming sensitized again. I feel close enough to Jessica to confide in her. I lean against the counter. "I don't know. . . . It just kills me how some people have it so easy — while others have to struggle for everything they get." It's so unfair, just thinking about it makes me scowl.

"Yeah. Ain't that something!" she

s. "How old are you now, Alicia? Six-
?" I nod. "So it's not like you're just
ding that out," Jessica says.

"No," I murmur.

"Knowng it is one thing. Coming to
terms with it is a little harder. Back home
in New Orleans," she reminisces, "I used to
go to hear these jazz musicians play in the
Quarter. In a place called Preservation
Hall. And take it from me, as black guys
living in the South before the civil rights
era, none of them had it easy. A lot of them
were old; most of them had no money. They
were well known in the Quarter, but none
of them ever became a household name —
a star if you like. But as musicians, they
were the real thing. All of them were first-
rate. They enriched the lives of all those
lucky enough to hear them." Jessica's voice
is as calm and low as ever. Yet she's speak-
ing with such passion. She holds onto her
memory of them for a few seconds longer.
Then she breaks the spell. "I figure if those
guys managed to become musicians," she
says briskly, "if they could maneuver their
way around the obstacles facing them, then
so could you — if your music is important
enough to you," she challenges.

I flare up defensively. "Just because you

give something up, people automatica... assume it wasn't important to you. Bu they don't have the right to do that," I protest. "They don't know how you're feeling inside."

Boy, for someone on novocaine, I sure sound wired.

Jessica looks concerned. "It's not that I don't sympathize with you, Alicia," she says gravely. "I do. Very much. That's why I'm nudging you to think twice about your decision."

"But it's too late," I wail.

"Of course it isn't, Alicia," Jessica replies. "Right now, time is on your side. But it won't always be," she warns. "You know what I've found out with time? People generally come to terms with the gambles that didn't work out. It's the risks they *didn't* take that haunt them. It's a little like being in limbo. Not a very good feeling if you ask me."

I look at her helplessly. When I walked in here, I thought I knew my own mind. Now I'm back where I started.

Jessica takes pity on me. "I don't mean to pressure you, Alicia. But you might give a thought or two to the things I've said today."

I roll my eyes. *Yeah, sure. Give a thought r two. Like when I'm staring at my ceiling, trying to fall asleep, for example. Jessica, don't you realize what you've done? You've said enough to give me insomnia for the next five years.*

Chapter 19

I sure have a lot of time to kill now that I'm not working at the Great Wave or composing songs. Yet somehow I don't have any more energy than I did before. If anything, I have less.

On Sunday, Mama and I go to mass at Holy Redeemer. The priest's sermon is about accepting your lot in life with grace. Mama nods solemnly throughout it, like she'd never heard it before. Which is definitely not the case. Resignation is a major theme at Holy Redeemer. It's given much more play than, say, mustering your courage to go for the brass ring. But familiar or not, I have to admit the priest's words have a calming effect on me. For better or worse, it looks like the roller coaster ride that began on Wednesday has finally come to a halt.

The apartment seems smaller than ever. Mama's going out of her way to be nice. To tell you the truth, though, I sort of miss her sarcasm. It used to keep me on my toes.

Evenings, I mostly hang out on the stoop. On summer nights our block is packed with people. There must be a thousand people living here — and each one has a story. Enough to fill four daytime soaps, easily. I never admitted it, but I used to dig getting the latest scoop on everyone from Mrs. Reuben. Lately, though, my curiosity is on a par with my energy level.

One night I'm sitting there staring into space when Mrs. Reuben sticks her head out. "I don't mean to be nosy, Alicia," she says. "But is your guitar broken?" Before I can answer, she continues, "I got my check from the Social Security this morning. So if you need to borrow to get it fixed, I'll offer you very reasonable rates." She smiles.

I'm really taken aback. Her offer is incredibly generous. "Thanks, Mrs. Reuben. But it's not broken."

"Then how come I never hear you play anymore?" she asks.

Needless to say, this is the very last topic I care to discuss. "I don't have time for it,"

I answer. From her expression, I realize I'm going to have to give her a few more details before she'll let me off the hook. "I'm studying to be an accountant," I volunteer.

But this only makes her look more puzzled. "Well, you have to do what you have to do," she says finally. "But to tell you the truth, I'm kind of sorry. I always enjoyed your songs."

She's got to be kidding. Maybe she enjoys the finished product. But how could she possibly have enjoyed the thousand and one wrong chords I subjected her to before I finally hit on a melody? "I used to be afraid I was bothering you," I admitted.

"Bothering?!" She arches her eyebrows in surprise. "Just the opposite," she claims. "You brightened my day."

Now it's my turn to look incredulous.

"I never told you?" she says. "I always meant to. It gave me so much pleasure — to hear you start out with just one line at first, and then working at it little by little until whoof — a whole new song," she exclaims. "And with such imagination."

Am I hearing this straight? Does Mrs. Reuben actually believe an imagination is a positive trait?

"Don't get me wrong. Accounting is a

very good profession. But to be as creative as you are — it's nothing to sell short," she says firmly.

I'm probably making a big deal over a few kind words, but Mrs. Reuben makes me feel like I've added something to her life. I remember Jessica's words about the jazz musicians at Preservation Hall. Maybe becoming a star isn't really the main thing. After all, that's a fluke. It involves so many things outside your control, like being at the right place at the right time and being in sync with pop music trends. The way things are set up in this country, even great talents don't always make it to the top.

So maybe what really matters is knowing that my songs had an effect on the people who did get to hear them. I don't know why I'm thinking about these things now. I mean, my mind is made up. . . . Or is it?

"Now let me see." Mrs. Kvares scans the various forms cluttering my desk. "We have the night school application, the medical insurance forms, and the pension plan. I guess that about covers it for now."

"I certainly hope so," I quip. But I don't feel nearly as lighthearted as I sound. Mrs.

Kvares has given me tons of forms to fill out. I don't know where to start. As I stare at them in a muddle, it hits me with a thud. Taking Junior up on his offer involves more than giving up my music. In fact, that was only a starting point. Nor does it involve simply signing up for a few night school courses at Baruch. Or setting up a part-time work schedule for the fall. No, going along with Junior's game plan means nothing less than adapting a whole new way of life. It involves my transformation from Tillie the Transient Temp to Miss Permanent Solid Citizen. Temps, after all, are just passing through. Perms, on the other hand, made this country what it is today.

"Have you decided on the pension plan you want?" Mrs. Kvares asks.

"Type A," I improvise. It was purely a wild guess. I haven't given the pension plan a single glance. As it turns out, she approves of my choice.

I pick out a form at random and start filling it out. I work with all the gusto of a snail.

"Well, I guess this is it," Mrs. Kvares comments. "You're becoming a lifer." I realize she's joking — sort of. Her words send shivers up and down my spine.

* * *

On Thursday, I get a postcard from Robin. It throws me for a loop. She's flipped out for one of the busboys — Sal Positano from Bridgeport, Connecticut. It's hard to believe, but she sounds almost ... *mushy*. All the same, it gets me thinking about my dateless state.

To be frank, it isn't a boyfriend that's uppermost in my mind. For the past two days, I've been fighting this urge. Just when I'm fairly sure I have it licked, it creeps up on me again. Oh, what's the harm, I say to myself. One little verse won't hurt anybody. I wonder how many hopeless alcoholics said the same thing about one little drink before they tumbled off the wagon. I take out my note pad and sneak a look at the random scribblings I've made in my spare moments. As if that's not reckless enough, I start humming a tune in my head. Next thing I know, I've edged my way to the closet.

I pause by the door and count to ten, but I don't turn back. Instead, I open the door. Calmly and deliberately, I take my guitar out from under the pile of clothing where I'd buried it. I could pretend I didn't know how it got there. I could pretend that, like a sleepwalker, I snapped out of my trance and suddenly found my-self with my guitar in hand. I could pretend I didn't know what I was doing. But I'd be lying. I settle down to compose my latest song. *Two Week Lifer*.

Chapter 20

From then on, there's no turning back. It's that simple.

Saturday morning when Mama returns from the supermarket, she calls to me from the kitchen. "Alicia, your registration from the night school came in the mail." She sounds real chirpy.

I tense. It's now or never, I decide on the spot. I try to rev myself up for the summit conference that's about to take place. The one Mama doesn't even know is on the agenda yet. I'm acting on my own for a change. There've been no pep talks from Steve, no rehearsals or strategy sessions, and Aunt Yo isn't on the premises to cushion the blow. No, this will be strictly a duet: Alicia to Inez.

I enter the kitchen and corner Mama by the refrigerator door as she puts a carton of eggs away. "I have to talk to you," I tell her.

"Talk," she shrugs. But when she glances at me, she realizes I have something major on my mind. She closes the refrigerator door and gives me her full attention.

I deliver the news calmly. "I just can't do it, Mama. I can't give up my music."

"Alicia, don't give me a heart attack," she interrupts angrily. "Besides, you already promised Mr. Miller," she points out. I guess in her eyes that makes it final. Not in mine, though.

"Monday, I'll have to tell him I've changed my mind."

Mama tenses and arches her neck, like a cat alerted to danger. It's dawned on her that getting me to back down isn't going to be a cinch. "It's only been two weeks," she coaxes. "You've got to give yourself a little more time to get used to it, Alicia."

"It won't make any difference," I explain. "I made a mistake. And now's the time to pull out — before classes start." My tone remains even, but there's a greater urgency behind my words.

"But what will Mr. Miller say?" my mother whimpers. As if that were the main consideration. She looks really jarred. Don't let her throw you, I tell myself. But as I re-state my case, I realize that a note of hysteria has crept into my voice. "Mama, I gave it my best shot. But it's just no good. I miss my music too much."

She scrutinizes me warily. I'm determined not to weaken under her stare. "It's *my* life, Mama." I'm practically begging for understanding. But instead of softening, Mama draws herself up coldly as she prepares to strike. "So because it's your life, I'm supposed to sit back and let you ruin it?" she retorts with icy sarcasm.

Something inside me snaps. "Why can't you believe in me?" I shout. My mother flinches. I've never raised my voice to her like this before. But I still want an answer to my queston. *"Why?"* I repeat.

"Because you're a dreamer with no common sense — just like your father."

I freeze. My mother turns away. I think about all the times I'd tried to get her to talk about Papa. It would have meant so much to me if she had said something — anything. At long last, she's broken her silence, I think bitterly. *At least Papa had a dream,* I feel like shouting.

Mama sits down at the kitchen table. She looks so sad and lost that it's hard to stay angry with her. I can tell she's sorry. But she can't just wish her words away. She has to do a little explaining. She owes me that much and she knows it. She stares at her hands for a few seconds. "Always, all his life, one big idea after another," she says wearily. "A band he managed — half the time they don't show up. A car service — with the cars always breaking down." Mama sighs as she remembers that episode. "And each time, we end up more poor than when we started out." Her voice isn't bitter, just sad. It's as if Papa's situation was too pathetic for her to resent him. "He thought because he believed so hard in his dreams, they had to happen. But it doesn't work that way." She pauses for a moment, then lowers her eyes. "You're the same way, Alicia. That's why I'm afraid for you."

I know she's said these last words not to hurt me, but because she really is worried about me. Only she's sold me short. "I'm not the same way, Mama," I try to assure her. "I'm not like that at all." She looks skeptical, but I can't take the time to argue. There are too many things I have to do.

Monday morning bright and early, I have a confidential talk with Miller, Junior to let him know about my change of heart. "I don't exactly know how to tell you this,

Mr. Miller," I begin. I'm lying. By this time, I'm such an old hand at quitting, it no longer fazes me. I know exactly how to tell him and that's exactly what I do.

Maybe I lay it on a bit thick. But then, turnabout is fair play. After expressing my gratitude at the generosity of his offer, I inform him regretfully that as far as Miller and Son is concerned, I'm strictly pinch-hitter material. He needs a steady bunter, at minimum. Then I become very apologetic about all the inconvenience I've caused him. When I wind down, I drop a few hints that I'd love to hold onto my part-time job — on a strictly temp basis. I know it's nervy of me, but I got my system down now. The gig's practically a piece of cake, and I need the salary. If I want to matriculate as a music major next year, I'd better start stashing away some dough. Junior's been a real good sport so far, so I don't want to press him too far. When he tells me to come around again once I know my fall class schedule, I thank him and beat it out of his office.

After work, I start making the rounds of the city colleges. Before long, I've picked up stacks of brochures. The cool spell we've been promised has failed to materialize.

Yet despite the heat, I've suddenly got energy to spare.

I talk to a couple of college counselors. They're very helpful. By this time, I have enough data to start making detailed plans. Plans A, B, and C, respectively. I calculate budgets for each of them. I figure out how many hours I have to work to come up with the tuition at each school. I estimate my weekly expenses.

Since our summit conference the past Saturday, things have been pretty chilly between Mama and me. But Friday night, she seems a little more relaxed. As she sits on the couch, I even notice her cracking a smile at some dumb joke the announcer on the Spanish language radio station has just told. I decide to go for it.

After offering only token resistance, Mama agrees to listen to a summary of my plans. Between a part-time job and a few nights at the Great Wave, I'll be able to swing city college tuition. I point out that a degree in music will qualify me to teach. To be blunt, I don't just point it out; I underline it. Mama seems relieved to hear this. I feel she's beginning to acknowledge there's a possibility, if just a slim one, that I may not end up in Potter's Field after all.

"See, Mama, I told you I wasn't just a dreamer," I boast as I conclude my presentation. Her expression remains passive. "You know . . . like you said Papa was," I add hesitantly.

I can feel her tensing. "Don't get me wrong. He always meant good," she says stiffly. I realize it still bothers her that she put him down to me.

"I know, Mama," I reassure her.

"It was very hard for him, Alicia. He saw everybody else get ahead. And he thought to himself, 'Why not me?' "

"Still," I comment, "it's like you said, wishing for things doesn't make them happen." She doesn't respond. It dawns on me that she hasn't said anything about my plan. I didn't expect a firm yes right off the bat, but I'd like to get some inkling of how I'm doing. I thrust one of my worksheets in front of her. "But here it is — in black and white, Mama. I can afford to send myself to college. I'll get by. I just have to cut a few corners."

Mama sighs. " 'Get by. Cut a few corners,' " she repeats wearily. "It's not the life I want for you!"

"It won't be forever."

She smiles wistfully. "How can I make you understand, *niña*? You think people

have children so they can say no to them?"
She pauses for a second. "When you were
a little baby, in the morning, you never
cried. Instead, you woke up singing. Your
Papa and I — we couldn't get over it." She
looks at me tenderly. She's never spoken to
me like this before. "I would like nothing
better than to say to you, 'Alicia, sing.' "
Mama's voice is strong but her eyes are
misty.

She means it, too, I say to myself in
amazement. I feel as if an enormous boulder
has been lifted from my shoulders.

Then my mother frowns and turns busi-
nesslike on me. I knew it was too good to
be true. "But what I learn from life, the
only thing I can say with my conscience
clear is *Niña, you got to be practical.*' "

"Mama, I *am* being practical," I insist.
"With a B.A. in music education, if I don't
find jobs singing, I can always teach."

She remains unconvinced. "What happens twenty years from now?" she asks. "If
you wake up and think, 'I gave up everything — and for what?' " She looks
straight into my eyes. "I don't want you
to know what that's like — to feel
cheated." Her manner is resigned, but her
eyes are bitter. They chill me.

I lean back. There's something I need to

explain to her, but it doesn't come easy. We're usually so guarded with one another. Exchanging confidences with her is like being in another country. "Sometimes at school, I get jealous of kids who have fathers," I begin. "You know, kids who have things easier. But when I play my music, I don't want to trade places with anybody."

I've purposely been avoiding her eyes. But now I feel I have to risk it. My mother is listening attentively. Her expression has regained the softness it had earlier.

"See, Mama, I'm not saying my songs are great or anything. But I'm the only person who can write them. That ought to count for something." When I started talking, I wasn't sure where I was going. Now I am. "So I have to go on with my music, Mama — no matter how you feel. But it would mean a lot to me if you could be on my side."

It's funny. Now that I've finally been able to talk to her honestly, I'm less afraid of her answer. Mama is silent. Just a little while ago, that would have made me nervous. But now it's okay. The strain between us has eased. I'm no longer hanging on her approval. Maybe because I feel that deep down inside, she's already given it to me.

Chapter 21

Before I go to bed I take out a snapshot
of Mama that was taken when I received
my First Communion. She has this proud,
happy grin on her face. I guess things were
pretty rocky between her and Papa at
times. But you sure couldn't tell by the
photos of her taken when he was still alive.
She looks almost radiant in some of them.

I smile. Mama's a character all right.
Steve may have had me in mind when he
said, "Some were born to brood," but that's
only because he didn't know Inez Rosa
Marin well. I'm convinced even Inez doesn't
know Inez well. Want to know why? For
years, she's tried to tell me in a million and
one ways, "*niña*, you got to be practical."

But at the same time, she was giving me
another message. It was always there, even

if it didn't come through clearly. But then, how could it? Mama herself didn't know what she was trying to say. She still doesn't. But I do. I've finally been able to cut through all the other stuff, and to get to the heart of the matter.

Mama's real message to me has always been, "Alicia, sing!"

> "You always stepped aside,
> So someone else could fly.
> You never tried your wings,
> But you opened up my eyes.
>
> It's as if you always knew,
> Someday, I'd sing this song
>   to you.

It's my first night back at the Great Wave. I didn't realize how much I'd missed it. It's like coming home again, and the people I'm singing to are just like members of the family. One of them is, in fact. And the song I'm singing is for her. For my mother Inez, who is sitting in the back letting her espresso grow cold as she hears me perform for the first time.

For heaven's sake, she looks so proud it's embarassing. Any moment now, I expect her to nudge one of the Gang of Four who are seated close by and boast, "That's my daughter, the singing waitress."

"A dream is only what you give it,
It won't last until you live it."